Gabriella

The Devil's Daughter Series: Book 1

Franki Zeal - Zani

ISBN:1985243512
ISBN-13:9781985243514

DEDICATION

To: All the people who were abusive and cruel, my biological father tried to kill me on several occasions, all the biological relatives who were supposed to love me but threw me away, everyone who ever told me that I was worthless and stupid, that I would never amount to anything and told me women were only good for one thing.

You were wrong. I am alive. You couldn't kill me. You couldn't break me. You broke bones, but you didn't break me. You don't own me. I owe you nothing. Don't come around, I don't need or want you in my life.

CONTENTS

Acknowledgements

I want to thank all the people who helped make this book possible. They encouraged me see possibilities when I couldn't find hope in myself. I believe that friends are the family you chose.

When my family threw me away my friends were there to offer love, compassion, encouragement, and **respect**. So, to all my friends a.k.a. (my mutually adopted siblings): I love you guys. You mean the world to me.

Chapter 1: Sweet 16

July 31st, 1975

My name is Maria Gabriella Cortez and today is my 16th birthday. Every year since I learned to write my mother has given me a diary. I always write about all the special things that happen to me. Mama says I will want to look back and remember the things that were important to me when I was young.

Today will be better than my Quinceañera. Nothing I get today will be as good as Marta's, but she is the oldest and Papa's favorite.

Marta is so beautiful and so smart. I want to be like my sister when I grow up. She is 18 now and a senior. She is very popular.

I told Marta for my birthday I would like to go to a dance club with her. She gets to go all the time. I just want her to take me once. She said no. She said I am too much of a little girl and I would spoil her fun. I told Marta I wouldn't. That I will do what she does and make her proud of me. But she just said I was stupid. I am going to ask Papa to make Marta take me. I just want to go once.

I asked Papa if for my birthday he would make Marta take me to the club. At first, he said I was too young, but I reminded him that Marta has gone every weekend since she turned sixteen. Besides my grades are better than Marta's and I always do what I am supposed to do. I will behave, only drink water, and make him proud. He said he would tell Marta. I'm so excited.

The party was beautiful. We had it in the back yard. Papa rented tables and chairs. We had waiters and waitresses. Every table had flowered centerpieces of White Lilies, Pink Azaleas, Blue Bells, and white Baby's Breath. It smelled so beautiful.

We had appetizers then salad. We had a lovely

dinner of orange chicken twice baked potatoes and vegetables. For dessert a white cake with six tiers and Azaleas made from frosting that looked like flower vines. It was so beautiful. The cake was strawberry, my favorite. We also had Vanilla Bean ice cream and Flan. It was all so delicious.

My cousin Roberto's band played. They are high school boys, but they were very good. Many of my relatives were there. I always ask for books for my birthdays, but no one ever gets me any. Some of my family gave me jewelry but many gave me money like at my Quinceañera. I have put the money in my hiding place. My jewelry too.

My dress was pink like an Azalea. The arms and bottom half of the skirt were light pink, and the bodice and top half of the skirt were deep pink. The skirt had layers and was flowy like you see in the Fred Astaire movies. The sleeves were full and puffy but made out of some gauzy material. I felt like a movie star.

I danced with all of my cousins. I wish I could have invited cute boys from school, but Papa says birthdays are only for family. I couldn't even invite my girlfriends from school. Everything was beautiful.

At the end of the party Marta and Papa were arguing near the house. He grabbed her arm and she yanked away. People started looking so Papa told the band one more dance. I hoped it wasn't about me.

I was helping Mama clean up and I walked under Marta's window. I saw Marta and Papa. He had one hand around her neck and the other was in her hair and it looked like he was shaking her. They were standing right by the foot of her bed. I ran to Mama and showed her, but she said, "It is between your father and Marta. It is none of your business. Get back to work." I started working again but I was afraid. I had never seen Papa like that. I was afraid for Marta.

Marta came to me after we were done cleaning up from the party. Her hair was still wet from her shower. She said she would take me next Saturday night to the club. She said she had things to do this weekend that had already been planned.

I asked Marta about what I saw. I told her that I told Mama, but she said it was none of my business. "She would." She said. Marta asked me if I understood what I saw. I told her what I thought. "You have so much to learn." She said. She looked mad for a minute when she said it. She told me to be ready Saturday night by six o'clock.

I'm so excited. I can't wait to tell my friends tomorrow. They will be so jealous!!

I can't decide what dress to wear. Do I wear my white one from my Quinceañera? Or my pink one from my birthday? Do I wear the green on from Mama and Papa's anniversary?

August 3rd, 1975

Mama came to me today and explained that dance clubs have people of many ages. I must be careful to only dance with boys my own age. I must never take drinks from strangers only from the bartender. "And above all never leave the main floor except to go to the bathroom. Do Not go into private rooms or away from the dance floor alone. Stay close to Marta. Bad *things happen to girls who wander off by themselves. "*

I promised Mama to do as I was told. But now I am afraid. What if something bad happens to me. Maybe I shouldn't go. I went to Marta and asked her if I should go. I told her what Mama said.

"You had better go after everything that happened." I didn't understand what she meant. I asked her about it, but she wouldn't tell me. Instead she said, "I go all the time and nothing bad has ever happened to me. Don't be such a little coward." Then she walked away.

August 9th, 1975

I was already dressed in my pink dress from my birthday when Marta came into my room. She had a red dress she wanted me to wear. It was so beautiful. It hugs my body, but I can still walk in it. It's not a girl dress. It's something a woman would wear. I feel so grown up. Marta had me put a shawl on over my dress. She said Papa would never let me leave the house otherwise.

Chapter 2: Betrayal

August 11th, 1975

Marta's friends had picked us up and drove us to the club. At first, I was excited and amazed by everything. It was a beautiful August evening. I ordered a water to drink while I listened to the music and got used to things. Several men came to ask us to dance. But I kept refusing.

"Why did you get Papa to make me let you come if you are not going to dance?" asked Marta.

"I want to dance but only with people my own age, like Mama said."

"Little coward. Good girls never have any fun." Marta replied. Then she went off to dance with a man much older than her.

Right after that a man came to the table and said, "Senor Ruiz wants your company."

I asked him to point out Senor Ruiz and he pointed to a man who had to be almost 30. I said no thank you I only dance with boys my age and went back to drinking my water.

I finished my water and went to the ladies' room. When I got back to the booth Senor Ruiz was sitting with Marta. He was sitting very close to her, with his arm around her. He was whispering in her ear and she was smiling and playing with the buttons on his shirt. I was shocked.

"Marta what are you doing?" I hissed at her.

"I am having a drink with Senor Ruiz. He works with Papa."

"I have never seen him at the drugstore." I said.

Senor Ruiz laughed, like I told a funny joke.

"That's because I don't work for your father. We are, sort of … partners."

"I have never heard Papa mention you." I didn't believe him. I stood up, it felt safer.

"Does your Papa tell you everything. Come. Sit. Let me get you a drink."

"No, thank you. Marta, I think we should go find another table."

"Little Coward. Go if you want to. But I will not be rude to a friend of father's."

Then I felt ashamed. Marta was right about me being rude. But I could not help it. Senor Ruiz was a strange man to me and I was afraid of him. I walked to where Marta's friends were talking to boys our age.

I got asked to dance by a boy named Alberto. He was 16 like me. He seemed very nice. I wanted so much to enjoy the dance but all I could think about was Marta sitting next to a man that scared me.

After the dance I went back to the table, where Marta and Senor Ruiz were looking very serious about whatever they were discussing. I apologized for being rude asked to join them. I sat on the very edge of the seat as far away from the both of them as I could get.

Senor Ruiz complimented me on my dancing. I thanked him. He kept trying to talk to me, but I kept looking at the table and at the clock behind the bar. Marta said we would leave by 11o'clock.

"Marta, it is almost 11. We should get the other girls and get ready to go."

"I want to have one more drink. Will you get it for me? I'll watch your water. Go ask for a Virgin Strawberry Daiquiri."

"A WHAT?" I was shocked at her language.

"It's a fruit drink. Virgin means no alcohol."

I did as I was bid. When I got back to the table Marta was holding my drink and stirring it with the straw. She drank her drink slowly. I finished my water quickly and excused myself to go to the bathroom. As I was walking things seem to go out of focus. I got so dizzy. I reached out and Marta was there, my big sister looking out for me.

"Come. Let's get you to the bathroom."

After we left the bathroom she walked me

through a door to a room. "What're weee doin' here? Not s'posed to go in a roooom. Mama sssaid. Not s'pose. I'm dizzy." Marta dumped me on something soft.

"I am going to enjoy this." A man said.

"First, where's my money? Thank you. Well, she's not going to be Papa's favorite anymore."

I reached for Marta but couldn't speak. Everything went black.

I woke up in a room I didn't know. I heard water running. I hurt everywhere. The light coming through the windows was very bright. My dress was on the floor. My underclothes were torn. There was blood between my thighs. I knew what happened then. I couldn't even think the word a good Catholic girl is not supposed to say.

I could barely move. I got my dress on, grabbed my shoes, and headed for the door. The water stopped.

"Ah, you're up. Shall we go again before I take you home?"

All the sudden I felt like I was freezing. I knew that voice although I only met him once. Senor

Ruiz was the man that attacked me.

I unlocked the door and walked out of the room, his mocking laughter ringing in my ears. I wanted to throw up. I came into an office. I walked through it into a hallway. I kept going. Through the other door it opened to the club. I tried to get out the front door, but it was locked. I saw an emergency exit on the other side of the room. Senor Ruiz came out of the hallway door. I ran for the club's exit. An alarm went off as I opened the door, but I still heard him laughing. I ran up the alley, past the garbage cans to the nearest street. I put my shoes on and started walking the way I thought was home. There was a convenience store on the next corner.

I asked them to call my father and I waited for him to come pick me up. I tried to talk to him, but he told me not to speak until we got home. When we got into the house the whole family was in the dining room.

"Your sister told us what happened. How could you bring such shame to the family? Did we not raise you better? Eh?! Drinking alcohol! Dancing with any man that asked you! Letting them touch you! Acting like a whore! How dare you!!" I was in shock. Didn't my family know me? I would never do such things.

I looked at Marta. Her head was down but she had a little smile on her face. In that moment I knew for certain she did this. I had not dreamed it. She did it all on purpose. Her choice. I didn't want to believe it before. My heart broke.

"It's a lie Papa, all of it. I only drank water. I only danced with 1 boy, 1 dance and he was my age. His name was Alberto. Marta was sitting with a man called Senor Ruiz. He said he was your partner. I was afraid for her. I didn't want to leave her alone with him. Someone put something in my drink. I felt dizzy and sick. Marta helped me to the bathroom and then took me to a room and left me there. She got money for me. Senor Ruiz attacked me. He was in the room when I woke up. I didn't do anything wrong. He hurt me." I was crying now. Papa walked up to me. I thought he would embrace me and make it all better like he did when I was a child. I imagined he would go and shoot Senor Ruiz.

Instead he slapped me across the face. "You act like a *puta* then tell lies on your sister and Senor Ruiz. When did you become so evil? Whore! Go to your room!"

I ran to my room and cried myself to sleep. I awoke when I heard a car door shut. I heard our doorbell, then voices talking.

I looked over the banister to the hall downstairs. I saw father invite Senor Ruiz into the dining room. I was terrified. I ran into my room and shut the door and hid like a child under my blankets and cried again.

Mama came and got me. She took me down to the dining room. "I have good news!" Papa said. "Senor Ruiz has admitted you were a virgin. He says he thought you were not because of the way you were acting. However, has generously offered to take you in marriage so that you may be forgiven in the eyes of God."

"NO! I will not marry that man! He lies! He attacked me! I... I will go to the police!"

"You have shamed this family and shamed yourself! You act like a slut to trap a man. Then when Senor Ruiz finds out you are a virgin he makes you an honorable offer. You will not stay in this house. You will go to live with Senor Ruiz either as his wife or as his whore. Your choice! But if you are not married you will no longer be welcome in this house, ever. You will be disowned!"

"Mama, pleeeease! You know I would not do this thing I am accused of. Mama!" I ran to my mother's arms, my last hope.

She pushed me away gently but firmly. "You are not the first woman to have an arranged marriage. Senor Ruiz is a wealthy man and can take care of you. What more can a woman ask for?"

Then she looked at me and her eyes were so dead inside. I was shocked into silence. I looked at my father then my mother. How could I be so blind? Had it always been like this and I was too much of a child to see? Did she go through the same thing? I walked out of the room.

At the top of the stairs I met Marta coming down. "How much Marta?"

"$200.00 but I would have done it for free. Now you know what Papa does to me. At least your virginity went to a stranger."

I ran for the bathroom and threw up. This is a house of evil secrets, a house of lies. How is it I never knew? What of the other children?

I got my money and my jewelry out of my hiding place. I went to my room, changed my clothes, and put the clothes from last night into my school book bag along with my diary and climbed down the tree that grew by my window.

I went to the police station and told them the truth. They took the dress I wore last night and the underclothes I had been wearing. They took me to the hospital and doctors examined me and did tests on me and took the clothes I wore the night before. Nurses helped me bathe and put me in a gown and put me to bed. They gave me medicine and I slept.

They police came to me the next morning and said they spoke with my father and he told them I was lying to cover up my own shameful behavior. They tore up the report in front of me and said I could go to jail for filing a false police report. They warned me not to do it again. I cried. No one believed me.

I hate 1975.

Chapter 3: Slave

My father picked me up when the doctor released me. He took me to a house I had never seen. He walked me inside and there was a Priest standing next to Senor Ruiz.

I turned around and tried to run but two men blocked the door and grabbed me by my arms and held me there. My father walked up to the Priest and said, "She's pregnant. He is the father. I give her to Senor Ruiz, in the eyes of God, in marriage."

I screamed no, I do not, he's lying, and I am not pregnant the whole time. But I was ignored. Senor Ruiz said, "I accept."

The Priest said, "I now pronounce you man and wife."

He gave me to a devil, a demon masquerading as a man. *In the Eyes of God,* he says. I think I have just been brought to Hell on Earth.

They all signed papers and still no one listened to me. The man dressed as a priest left the house. "What did you get for me? Did you sell me like Marta?" I screamed at my father. Never in my life did I ever think I would talk to him that way.

"What are you giving my father?" I yelled at Ruiz.

"You have spirit. Good. I am going to enjoy breaking you in. Soon you will learn who is boss."

"I hate you!" I screamed at them both. Then I was silent. I had never said those words before. I had never felt those feelings before today.

"I am giving your father a raise in pay. He will be more prosperous than he is now."

"Father please don't do this. I didn't do anything wrong."

"I know." Then my father walked out the door. The two big men dragged me upstairs, threw me into a room with no windows and locked the door.

I had dreamed of my wedding since I was a child. This terrible thing that just happened is not a wedding. I cried myself to sleep again. This is not a marriage and I will never forgive my father for doing this to me.

Still August 1975, I think

When Senor Ruiz first came into the room I held on to my book bag for dear life. He laughed at me and said, "Keep your childish toys. I don't mind that you are still a little girl. In fact, I prefer it." I was suddenly freezing. I didn't know for sure what he meant but it didn't sound good.

He let me keep my school bag and my diary. I think he thinks it doesn't matter. He didn't even bother to look inside.

He has people bring food to me once a day I think. I tried to eat slow the first time, but they came and took the food away after only a few minutes. They wouldn't let me finish eating. Now I eat as fast as I can.

There is a bucket in this room and they bring me toilet paper when I am low. It is always dark in here, so I can't tell if it's day or night.

They let me out of the room today. Some men came in and held me down while Ruiz cut my clothes off me. They threw me in a shower and sprayed me with soapy water and hosed me down like an animal. They threw me back in the room and threw a dress in after me. I screamed and yelled and called them names the whole time. They just laughed at me.

Ruiz said, "You are so funny."

I am so ashamed. I wish I were stronger, so I could escape. I cried a long time.

September 1975, Maybe

He never lets me outside or near open windows unless they have bars and a lock. It's no use calling out. There are no other houses around. He beats me now. For no other reason than his own entertainment. He slaps me, so I will try to fight and then he beats me, so I will stop.

He doesn't break bones, but he makes me exhausted. Then he laughs at me. Sometimes he pees on me. I cry a lot. He feeds me three times a day now, but the meals are very small.

November 1975

It will be thanksgiving soon. I hear them talk about it on the radio. He raped me today after he beat me. I cried and threw up on him. He didn't give me anymore food today.

December 1975

He told me it was Christmas and he was going to give me a present. He took me to his bedroom and beat me there. He tied me face down on the bed when I was too tired to fight anymore. He did horrible things to me. It hurt very bad. Then he cut me in several places. I bled for a long time. I told him I hated him, and he would burn in Hell for his sins.

"But I gave you a present. You get to sleep in a bed now." He just laughed at me.

1977 I think

I have been here two years I think. He burned his name in my back today. I **HATE** him with all my heart. I wish he would **DIE**!

I was pregnant. He realized it before I did. He told me I was pregnant. Then he hit me over and over in the lower part of my stomach until I started to bleed. It hurt so bad.

He has not been to see me since I lost the baby. I hear screams from other parts of the house. I wish <u>I</u> would die. The things he does to me hurts so much.

I am so afraid. All the time. I wish I would just die, even if it was because he beat me to death.

1978 I think

He brought dogs home today. He said he rented them for me. I wonder if he will have them kill me.

I am alive, but I wish I were dead. He is sick and evil. What sort of person teaches dogs to do that to people? He asked me if I wanted a pony next. I told him to just kill me already. He said he couldn't do that because I was too much fun. He brought a doctor to the house to treat my wounds. Then he did things to me in front of the doctor.

Chapter 4: Hope

May 1982

Senor Ruiz's father is coming for a visit. He stopped hitting me in the face, so I would look good when his father shows up.

I don't know how he's going to hide my pregnancy. I don't know why he would let me keep this one. He has beaten four babies out of me I think.

Senor Ruiz got me a dress to wear for his father's visit. Mostly he just keeps me naked.

Senor Ruiz is very angry. His father decided to stay until the baby was born.

Manuel has taken his other slaves elsewhere. The house is so quiet it is frightening. Papa Ruiz told Manuel that he should stay in a different room until I deliver. Manuel is angry all the time, but he never touches me when his father is anywhere near me. Papa Ruiz is around me almost all the time. Sometimes I cry because I don't know how to act or what to do. Ruiz has never left me alone this long. I am glad I am healing but am scared of what will happen when Papa Ruiz leaves.

When Ruiz gets restless he goes away for the day and leaves more guards at the house. When he comes back he is happy. I think that he must be visiting his slaves wherever they are.

I think Papa Ruiz is different than his son. Papa Ruiz and I talk and take walks in the garden. He taught me to play chess. He has me sing for him. We play cards. He never leaves me alone with Manuel. I eat better than I ever have with Manuel. Papa Ruiz insisted that I be moved in the room next to him. I keep my school bag and my journal with me everywhere I go, I write and draw. Papa Ruiz asked to read the journal. He never said anything, but his face got very tight. Like angry maybe? I have hope.

I asked Papa Ruiz to take me and the baby with him when I deliver. I told him that Manuel is cruel and evil. He has made it very clear that he wants the baby, not me. Women are useless he says. He is hoping for a grandson, "that he can take and raise better than he raised Manuel." I have lost hope for myself but maybe the baby will be safe.

I know now no help will come.

Chapter 5: Baby Doctor

September 6, 1982

I have never been to a baby doctor. Manuel always beat the baby out of me so there was no need before. Papa Ruiz insisted that I see one today.

It was the first time I was in a car since I was forced to live with Manuel. Papa Ruiz let me put the window down a few inches. Manuel said I looked like a dog with my face in the window taking deep breaths. He has called me far worse. I didn't care.

All the sights and sounds reminded me that there was an entire world out there. Maybe I wasn't so alone after all. It was easy to forget because Manuel's house is so far out of the city. There are no other houses near that I can see.

The doctor did an ultrasound on me and we saw the baby. I had never imagined such things. It's a girl. I was nearly 8 months. As soon as we got to the car Papa Ruiz blew up.

Papa Ruiz was furious. "This is all your fault! How many times has she lost babies that could have been my grand-son? You! Irresponsible! IDIOT!"

"Well, now you will have a grand-daughter instead." Manuel looked pleased and that scared me badly.

"What use is a girl child?! It can't take over the business. You should sell if for a profit like I did your sisters and try again." I was wrong. Papa Ruiz was also a devil, just a different kind.

"I am not ready for a son. I like the idea of a girl. I will raise it to obey me, serve me and do what I say without question. When it is old enough it will take Maria's place."

I still faced the window. It was a good thing. I could feel my face. I was terrified and disgusted. And I couldn't keep my face straight.

"Are you crazy? You could teach any of your pets to do this. But to do this thing with your own child, this is how insanity starts. Damn royals. Marrying cousins made them crazy and you want to do this with your own child?"

"Of course not. No babies will be made. I will have her fixed."

"Hmm. Well I suppose you think that's different. I still think you should sell her. Today's market for babies you get 50 thousand for my maybe."

"No."

We sat in silence the rest of the way home. I was in shock. I was terrified for the child. My poor daughter was doomed before she was born.

As soon as we got back to the house I headed for my room. "Where are you going?" I stopped on the stairs leading into the house.

"I was going to my room Papa Ruiz." I spoke quietly, respectfully, careful not to show any emotion on my face.

"Do you know how to cook?" I nodded. "Good. Go make us something to eat." I wasn't sure what to do. I knew with me carrying a girl, things had changed. I looked to Manuel.

He laughed. "Well you still remember who is boss eh? Good. Yes, go make the food little dog." He laughed again.

I didn't move. "I am sorry. I don't know where the kitchen is."

Then they both laughed. "At the end of the dining room is a door. Go through it. You will find the kitchen. In the kitchen are 3 more doors, a pantry, a bathroom, and a door to the sitting room. That is where Manuel and I will be."

"What do you want me to make?"

Manuel looked at his watch. "It's 9:30 now, have lunch ready by noon. I don't care what you make. Impress me and maybe I will let you out to cook more often."

"If you get hot there is a window you can open. My son does not believe in air-conditioning."

I put my head down and I went into the kitchen. I looked through all three doors. I used the bathroom and started pulling ingredients out of the pantry and refrigerator. As I was cooking I needed more light. I didn't see a light switch, so I decided to open the curtains.

Chapter 6: Escape

When I did, I realized it may be the key to my freedom. I looked out the window and didn't see any one outside. I turned the lock and very carefully opened the window. It opened all the way up. There was no screen. There was no breeze. I left the window open and shut the curtain.

Alberto, one of the guards, came walking through the kitchen. I stood very still. He grabbed an apple from the table and spoke very quietly. "You don't have to make a lot of food. Senor Ruiz's father thought it would be a good idea to send most of the guards home for the day. You know, give them a treat. It's pretty hot outside. After all, how could you know something like that. You would probably assume there were still a dozen guards around the house like normal. You know, if you turn on the bathroom light and fan and lock and shut the door it will seem like you are in there."

He walked over to the stove and turned it down. "If you add some water to this it will take longer to start burning. Give you more time. Good luck. You never deserved any of this. Now I can say when I came through last you were here." Then he walked out the door that led to the dining room biting the apple.

My legs felt like jelly. Did that really just happen?

I put some water in the pot and turned it down even further and gave it one last stir. I went quietly to the pantry and put food in my bag. I took fruit and a container of juice out of the refrigerator and put it in my bag. I got a couple of knives out of the drawer. He would not get me back without a fight. I went to the bathroom and turned on the light and the fan, then locked and shut the door.

I knew from my walks from Papa Ruiz that there were security cameras on the front of the house but not the sides or back. The guards were always spread throughout those areas. The sides and the back of the house had a very tall brick wall with decorative statues of different sizes every 10 feet or so. The house also had a wrap-around porch.

Directly across from the kitchen window was the horse with a mounting block.

Papa Ruiz had me get on it once, he seemed to find it funny. I had never ridden a horse in my life. I had a tough time getting on and Papa Ruiz showed me how to use the mounting block. I had thought it was a tree stump.

While I was on the horse I was very aware of how close I was to the top of the wall. I knew I would never get away with Papa Ruiz watching me. I told Papa Ruiz I thought I might be afraid of heights and asked for his help down.

As quietly as I could I went out the window onto the porch. No one was around. I shut the window as much as I could. I went over the porch railing and looked everywhere I could.

I climbed onto the "stump," then the horse, stood up and got on the wall. Then over the wall and hung off the other side by my fingers. I dropped and lost my footing and landed on my butt. I stayed close to the wall catching my breath. I was so afraid.

Then I realized that God must truly be smiling on me. Tall dark green grasses came almost up to the brick wall. I knew we were near a marsh or some swampy area, but I didn't realize just how close we were. My dress, a present from Papa Ruiz, matched the grasses almost perfectly. I unbuttoned my dress partway and pulled it up over my dark brown hair.

I crouched down and ran straight for the grasses.

The whole time I was running I tried to listen for alarms, or shouts, any sign that they knew I was gone. But all I could hear was my breathing and my heart pounding in my chest.

I ran until I fell. I took some time to catch my breath and then got up and started walking. I tried to keep the road in my sites while staying hidden in the grasses. I thought I remembered some of the turns that got us into the city. All I could hope for is to keep trying to get to a town.

I am trying to make my food stretch. I ate only once a day from the food I stole from Manuel. I also eat the fresh grasses, small green twigs, and all the seaweed that I can stomach from the beaches.

I think I am lost but Manuel still has not found me, so it must be good. I found a small neighborhood. It looked like it might rain so I stayed the night in a tree house.

A child found me in the morning. I asked the

little boy not to tell anyone I am here. I told him I was stolen and am running away from the bad man who took me. I told him when the rain stops I will go away. He said his name was Devon. He promised not to tell.

Devon brings me food and water every day. The rain didn't stop for 3 days. I was able to rest and write in my journal. I sneak down when the curtains are drawn in the window that faces the tree house. I use the bathroom in a field close by.

When the rain stopped Devon came out with his mother. I was terrified. Michelle, Devon's mom, told me that she didn't tell anyone I was here. She asked me where I am going. I told her I didn't know. Michelle sent Devon back into the house.

Michelle and I spoke for several hours. Michelle asked me lots of questions about what happened to me, where I was from and if there was anyone who could help me. I started to relax and felt safer than I had in a long time.

"The man that did all these things to you, where is he now?"

"Senor Ruiz? I don't know. Looking for me I guess."

"Ruiz? Manuel Ruiz?! The Drug Dealer! Oh my God. You have no idea what you brought here. We have to get you out. Stay here until I get Devon to someplace safe."

Michelle took Devon to a neighbor's house. Michelle took me into the house and I got a shower, fresh clothes, and a meal. While I was in the shower Michelle burned the green dress, underclothes, and shoes I ran away in. She asked I if she was willing to cut my hair. Michelle told me that I could get good money for my hair from a wig maker.

Michelle made copies of my diary and wrote down everything I had already told her. She also asked a bunch of new questions that she wrote down. She said she was going to send it all to a friend at the FBI. Michelle worked for the District Attorney's Office. She wanted to see Manuel Ruiz in jail almost as much as I did.

She put a pillow, a sheet, and a jacket in the back seat of the car. She also gave me a small suitcase on wheels. The suitcase had food and a couple of changes of clothes. Men's shirts and sweaters, that she said were her husbands, to cover my belly and a couple of skirts and some sweatpants. She gave me $300.00 and told me she was going to drive me to a different city, so I could get a bus out of town. I told her I had some money. Ruiz never looked in my schoolbag, so he never found it. She told me to take it anyway for the bus ticket.

I laid in the backseat and covered up with the sheet and slept some. Michelle passed through the nearest town without stopping. She pulled off the highway at a rest stop, so I could go to the bathroom. She pulled off the highway at another place to get gas. I stayed hidden.

Michelle went to a second city. She took me to a wig maker and helped me sell my hair. I was left with a short haired pixie cut. That's what Michelle called it. I thought the name was funny.

Michelle parked her car in a parking garage a few blocks from the bus depot. She went and got a round trip ticket in her own name to Atlanta, Georgia. She told me she has family there, so it wouldn't look strange. Michelle told me that when I got to Atlanta I needed to find someone at a homeless shelter to come back to

Florida by the end of the week. That was the only way to protect Michelle and Devon. I promised that I would. Michelle told me that if anyone asked for I.D. I should say that I lost my wallet.

I have decided if I can't find someone, then I will go back myself. I didn't want Michelle and Devon to be at risk. She left the parking garage and I walked the few blocks to the bus depot.

The bus driver said I should use the bathroom before getting on the bus. He said it would be difficult to use because I was pregnant, and the bathroom was small. It made me want to cry.

I was taught growing up to never trust strangers, only family. But random people were showing more concern for me and my baby than anyone had since I was betrayed by my own family. I stayed in the back of the bus out of sight thinking about my life. Not just my time with Senor Ruiz but my whole life and everyone and everything in it.

When I looked at my childhood with new eyes I realized so much more that had been wrong about my life and my family. In many ways my family was as troubling as the Ruiz's. I cried a lot on the bus.

Chapter 7: Atlanta

It was still dark when we got to Atlanta. I expected Senor Ruiz or his father to be waiting for me when I got off the bus. I was so scared that I ran off the bus and out the nearest exit.

I ran for a long time, ducked into an alley, and threw up. Then I used the bathroom in another alley. I left that alley and went to another alley, sat on a garbage can and cried. I don't know how long I cried, but the sun was up in the sky when I was done.

I started walking down the street looking for a restaurant. I got directions to a diner nearby. I got information from them and using a phone book got information on homeless shelters. From different shelters I found out where homeless people tend to gather.

I stayed in homeless shelters at night and searched for women during the day who might want a ticket to south Florida. It took me 5 days. I was scared that I might have to go back to protect Michelle and Devon.

The girl I found was 16. Her name was Tracy. She ran away from home when her mother's boyfriend raped her. So much ugliness in this world. I realize now how sheltered I had been.

Tracy had grandparents in Florida. She had and old birthday card but no phone number. The lady at the homeless shelter helped us contact Tracey's grandparents.

The grandparents were her father's parents. They lost track of Tracey and her mom after her father died and Tracey's mom got into drugs. Tracy's grandparents wanted her, they loved her. We told them where and when to pick Tracey up.

I got big sunglasses, wore the coat Michelle gave me, and wore different clothes than the ones I wore when I came in on the bus and left my suitcase in the office at the homeless shelter but took my school bag. I took Tracey to the bus depot and made sure she got on the bus. I went to a diner and used a payphone to call her grandparents and asked them to call me at the homeless shelter to let me know she arrived.

I was a so nervous the whole time I was waiting, I paced constantly. I was afraid she would get off the bus somewhere and I would still have to go back to Florida. Tracy's grandparents called me from the bus station as soon as she got off. I left the shelter after the phone call. I would be staying that night on the streets.

September 20, 1982

I went to a 24-hour diner. I was talking to a waitress, Lucy, about jobs that paid cash and didn't ask for I.D. because "I had lost my wallet." I was talking about the things I knew how to do when I felt a strange pain hit me. It felt like a bee sting in my back. I flinched, and Lucy asked if I was ok. I said I was fine.

Lucy said that a regular customer was looking for a housekeeper because he was out of town a lot on business. He wanted to make sure his apartment was safe and being looked after. I

45

must have looked nervous because the waitress said she dated the guy, but he was too sweet and old fashioned for her. She just wanted a fling and he was looking for something more serious. She said he was a total gentleman, very respectful and stayed friendly even after they stopped dating.

I told her I wanted to meet him someplace public. Lucy said he was in there that night. His name was Jason James. She pointed him out then, Lucy went to talk to him.

I looked up ready to run just in case and saw the man talking to Lucy. He was friendly, and he smiled a lot while talking to her. He looked clean but average. His clothes were not fancy. He looked up when Lucy pointed to me, he smiled, waved, and started talking to Lucy again.

Lucy walked away and came back to me. Lucy apologized to me and said that she was wrong. Jason wasn't looking for a maid anymore because he was being transferred to California.

I felt the baby kick right after Lucy said California. Then I felt a sharp pain in my stomach, and then it went quickly away.

Lucy asked me again if I was ok. I said yes, that I must be hungrier than I thought. So, I ordered soup and a salad to go with my hot chocolate.

I was drinking my hot chocolate when Mr. James walked up to my table. "Hi. I'm Jason. I'm sorry that I am not looking for a housekeeper anymore. I should have told Lucy since I asked her to help me find a nice person to be a live-in housekeeper and cook. Lucy has really good instincts about people and would never recommend someone that she didn't think would be a good fit though. So, I thought I should at least come and meet you."

"Person?"

"Sure. I'm not sexist. I don't care if it's a man or woman. I just want someone trustworthy."

My mouth was literally hanging open.

"What? Do you think only women should be housekeepers or cooks? My mother raised me and my brothers on her own. She had an important job and paid for nannies when she wasn't there. But she always kept a firm hand on all of us. She wanted us to know that women can do anything that men can do. Even at my age if she heard me disrespect a woman she would probably beat the crap out of me."

I started laugh, then cry. "I'm sorry. I just never heard any man talk about men and women as equals."

"Hey. Hey that's ok. Are you, all right?"

"I don't know. I am learning about a lot of different things in a very short time and I think it may be a little too much for me."

"Would you mind if I joined you?"

I looked to Lucy who was bringing my food and she said, "You know I don't get off until 8 a.m. so take your time eating. You look like you could use a few good meals."

"Alright, Mr. James, I guess so."

He reached out his hand to me, "Please call me Jason." I hesitated, then shook his hand and changed my life.

Chapter 8: Baby

I talked with Jason James all night. He told me about his upbringing in England, his military career, and his life in America. we talked about music and movies, books, and his hobbies.

Jason kept me laughing. He kept trying to get me to talk about myself, but I would ask more questions about him.

From time to time I would get pains and every time I did Jason would ask if I was ok. I was touched by his compassion for me. It was nearly 7 in the morning before I got really tired all of the sudden.

"Why don't you want to talk about yourself?"

"I, um, well I.... OH MY GOD!" I felt like my stomach was torn open. "I have to go." I put a 20.00 on the table for Lucy. I got up to leave. I slipped and would have fallen but Jason pushed the table with his feet and caught me. He was so fast and so gentle. He held me like I was made of glass. He gently helped me to my feet.

"Gabriella, you can't go anywhere, but to the

hospital. I am pretty sure your water just broke."

"NO!" I pulled away. "I CAN NOT go to a hospital!" I took a step and grabbed my suitcase and my bag. I was trying to walk away, and the pain hit again. "Arghhhh. Oh God." I doubled over.

"Gabriella, please, listen to reason. Your contractions are coming to close together. You need a hospital." He put his hand on my arm, but it didn't hurt me.

"NO!! If I go to a hospital he will find me. He will get me and the baby. He will kill me and do horrible things to her. No. No, I can't."

"What if I can guarantee that no one will find you? That you and the baby, will be safe."

"You can't. You don't know him like I do. He is EVIL. No one will listen to me. I am only a woman. No one cares." I yanked my arm away and tried to walk away, but the pain hit again, and I fell on the floor.

"That's it. I want to convince you, but you are just going to have to trust me." Jason picked me up so fast it took my breath away. "LUCY!"

She came running out of the back and saw Jason standing in baby water with me in his arms. "Where's your car?"

"Around the corner. I am going to go get it. Don't let her leave." Jason put me down on a seat near the front door. Lucy gathered my things and stood in front of me to block my way.

"I need to goooo! Pleeeease!" There was another pain and I was crying now.

"Look at me. He is a really good guy. I met him because he saved me from a couple of guys who robbed me then dragged me in an alley to rape me. I was walking home from work. He could have just kept jogging, but he didn't. He beat the crap out of them. Got someone to call the cops and then even went to the hospital with me so I wouldn't have to be alone.

When we dated he never even had sex with me because he didn't want me to feel obligated. He wanted to see if we clicked on our own before we moved to the next level. I'm 22 years old. I'm not ready to settle down and get married. I swear Gabriella, he is a good guy and he could protect you." I must have looked panicked because she said, "Sorry, I was eavesdropping." She smiled then, I smiled. I still had tears running down my face. I wish I had this relationship with my sisters. I found it sad that I had to experience this with a complete stranger, but grateful that I found it at all.

"Stuff." Jason stretched out his hands to Lucy for my belongings. He put them in his trunk, slammed it and opened the passenger door. He ran back into the restaurant. He didn't ask this time just picked me up and gently put me in the front seat.

As we drove to the hospital he asked me questions that he said he needed to know to keep me safe. I was afraid to answer. I thought about what Lucy said. I thought about how he had been with me all night. I decided to trust him. He was right. I needed a hospital. After I had the baby I could run again.

"Have you ever heard of the name Manuel Roberto Garcia Ruiz?" I looked at my hands in my lap gripping my skirt in fists. I was so scared I started sweating, or it could have been the pain from the baby.

"That crazy, drug guy in Florida? Yeah, he's been in the news, but they can't seem to catch him on anything."

"My sister sold me to him to be raped and told my family I went with him on purpose. My father said I would have to marry him. I ran away and went to the police and told them everything. The police talked to my father. Then they came to me while I was in the hospital bed and said I filed a false report and would go to jail if I did it again. My father took me out of the hospital and gave me to Ruiz and a priest said we were married and he and my father signed papers." I took a deep breath. Jason didn't say anything.

"That was August 1975. I was 16. Senor Ruiz didn't want a wife. He wanted someone that he could torture. I ran away after we found out I was having a girl. His father wanted him to sell the baby and get money. Senor Ruiz said he wanted to raise the baby and train her to be his new slave. He would kill me when she was old enough to take my place." I felt ice cold. I didn't know what to expect. He was dead silent. I looked at him.

Jason looked strange. It looked like he was grinding his teeth. He gripped the steering wheel so tight his knuckles were pure white. I was afraid he didn't believe me.

"You're right. I do need a hospital. You can drop me off I'll be ok."

"ARE YOU BLOODY INSANE??!!! NO, YOU WILL NOT BE OK! THERE IS NO WAY IN BLOODY HELL I AM LEAVING YOU TO FEND FOR YOURSELF AFTER WHAT YOU JUST TOLD ME! FOR THE LOVE OF CHRIST!" He was shouting in the car I flinched and cowered against the door.

"I'm sorry. I'm... I wasn't yelling at you.... It's just. I ... God... Hang on." He pulled down a street, stopped the car, put it in park, opened the door, leaned out and threw up in the street. I was so shocked I just sat in the car and watched until he was done. He took a handkerchief out of his pocket and wiped his mouth.

"Gabriella, I think that is literally the worst thing I have ever heard in my life. I am so sorry about what you went through. No one deserves that."

I burst into tears. Who was this man God put in my path? "I was afraid you didn't believe me."

"I believe you. I have seen some truly terrible

things as a soldier but imagining you…. God it's just…" When he looked at me, Jason had tears in his eyes. Maybe that was from throwing up. "Is there anything else I need to know right now."

"I have many scars. Do you need to hear the rest now?"

He looked at me in horror and spoke as quietly as he had shouted earlier. "The rest?"

"Yes."

"Not now. I have to drive to get you to the hospital." He started driving again.

"Maybe not. I think the pains have stopped." Jason started driving again.

"Uh, uh. Nope. No Ma'am. We are going straight to the Emergency Room. We are not taking any chances with your health. Ok. So, my name is Jason Bartholomew James. You are my wife. If people ask about your scars, we say you were kidnapped in Mexico on our honeymoon and I just got you back. My name will go on the birth certificate as the baby's father."

"NO! If he finds me he'll come after you too. I

can't let you do that for us."

"I was a soldier. I put my life on the line every day for God and country. This is the first time I get to make a difference I can see and touch. They put the mother's maiden name on the birth certificate not the married name."

"My name is Maria Gabriella Cortez."

"I like Gabriella."

"So, do I, it was my grandmother's name."

"Ok we'll stick with Gabriella. Maybe you should use her last name as well. To help hide you and the baby."

"Her maiden name was Diego."

"Good. A nice generic Spanish name."

"Generic? Owwwooooowwwha." Pains again.

"Generic. Common. We're here!" He got out of the car very fast and ran inside the doors. He came out with two men, a lady, and a rolling bed. He gave his keys to one of the men and got me carefully out of the car. He put me on the bed and we started to go inside as the man got in Jason's car.

"But, your car." I sat up.

"It's ok. I told the guy I would give him $20.00 if he parked my car and brought your bags from the trunk. I want to be here for you. It's ok. I promise. I will <u>NOT</u> leave your side."

And he didn't. Jason answered all the questions and stayed with me until I had the baby. She was early but healthy. He insisted that the baby stay in the room with us. The hospital didn't like it but finally agreed. We named her Angelica Marguerite Diego James.

He paid a security guard who was off duty to stay with me and the baby while he went to get us something to eat. He stopped at the gift shop on the way up. He got me some magazines, a deck of cards and a new journal. He also got a small stuffed green frog for the baby. He put it next to her. "It was the only thing they had left. Apparently, there have been a bunch of babies born and they haven't restocked the shelves yet. Do you think she'll like it?"

"I think she will like anything you give her." *And so, will I. I will remember all your kindness and tell her of you when you are gone.*

The rest of the day we talked about some of the world I had missed out on and played cards. The next day when we were ready to go he bought a car seat from the hospital and insisted we go home with him. I had nowhere else to go and I wanted to spend time with him before he left the state and my life forever.

Chapter 9: Safe

Lucy used to babysit and knew all about what babies need. Jason paid her to take time off work and stay with me while he went out and bought all the things for the baby she gave him a list for. He was afraid if left alone I would run like a scared rabbit. I think he was probably right.

Lucy also gave me and Jason instructions on how to care for a baby. Jason took notes like his life depended on it. He filled several notebooks. Jason bought all the books recommended by Lucy. He and I took turns reading them out loud to each other.

He put a lock on the bedroom door to help me feel safe and stayed on the couch. He took time off his job. When I was ready and able to get out of the house he took me shopping for clothes and things for me and the baby. I was scared about the amount of money he spent. I didn't want to be in his debt. But he shrugged it off and said he was ok. He could afford it.

Jason asked me to come to California with him. He worked really hard to try and convince me. He felt the further we were away from

Florida and Ruiz the better off we would all be. We talked all the time very late into the night and early morning. I told him everything about my life, even the stuff that wasn't in my diary. I felt I owed him that.

Ultimately it was how he treated us that convinced me. He would hold and rock the baby, change diapers, play with her, read, and sing to her and tell her stories. He helped with laundry, cooking, and housecleaning. He did beautiful little things everyday with her that my father never did with me or any of the other children.

He often made me cry with the sweet things he did for us. I couldn't help it; the tears would just come. But instead of making my head hurt or making my feel bad like they did with Ruiz, I felt like the tears were washing away the pain and the hurt and ugliness that came before, making room for the love in my heart that was growing for the Jason and the baby.

At first it was really hard for me. The baby was born with coal black hair and dark brown eyes. Every time I looked at her I would think of Ruiz and get so angry, I was afraid I would hurt her. So, it was Jason who mostly took care of the baby in the beginning.

Jason never made me feel bad about it. He told me that if I couldn't find a way to deal with it then maybe we should consider adoption, find her a home where she would be loved and protected.

I thought about it and decided that I couldn't put that on some stranger. What if Ruiz found her? He would just kill whoever had her and she would end up his victim. I decided I was just going to have to find a way to make it work.

When the baby was almost 2 months old everything changed. Her eyes were turning light brown and her hair was coming in red and brown. We took her to the baby doctor and he explained this was normal. Many babies are born with very dark eyes and even dark hair, but it changes as they grow. I was amazed. I felt like God was taking pity on me, trying to help me forget where she came from.

I finally agreed to go to California, 2 days before Jason was supposed to leave. I tried to give myself to him, but he refused.

"How can I possibly pay you back for everything you have done. What can I give you?"

"I don't expect you to trade yourself like that. Everything I have done is because I wanted to. You and Angie have wound your way into my heart and I love and care about you both. I am not in love with you, but I would do it all again in a heartbeat. You have been through hell and I would never take advantage of you that way. Maybe someday you might love me, and I might love you. But for now, maybe we should just try to be friends. Just be there for each other like a family should."

I agreed.

Chapter 10: Family

Jason insisted on paying me wages. I felt awkward about it at first, but Jason said if he had hired someone the way he intended he would be paying them and they would be living in the room that I shared with Angelica. He didn't see the difference. But I did and told him so. He pays for things for Angelica. To me that was the difference.

He said I should look at us like a family business. If he was my brother and owned a restaurant and I worked for him, I would still be getting wages. And would it be wrong for an uncle to get his niece nice things? He didn't think so. He also brought up the point that if anything happened I should have money of my own to take care of me and Angelica.

He made very good points, but I couldn't help but see the differences. So, in my diary at the back I kept track of everything he did for us financially. I was determined, that someday I would pay him back.

It was after we were in California for about a

week when Jason had to leave for the first time. He said he had to check in to his new post and new boss. Jason would be gone for three days. I was very nervous to be by myself with the baby. Jason had two months of practice. I had almost two weeks.

At first things were going well. But Angelica kept trying to look around and she did this little noise, almost like a call. Jason said it was the noise she made when she wanted to play or wanted company. So, I tried to play games and read and sing like Jason did, but it didn't work. She kept calling and looking around. Once she realized that Jason wasn't there she had this panicked look on her little face. Then she started to scream and cry.

Jason was gone for three days. It felt like years. By the time he got back I was hysterical.

Angelica wouldn't eat, wouldn't sleep. She cried, then would throw up from the crying. When there was nothing left in her stomach she dry-heaved. I would try to get her to take a bottle and she would choke. Jason came through the door and I was holding Angelica and she and I were both crying.

I jumped off the sofa, shoved the baby into

Jason's arms and ran back to the sofa and shouted, "She hates me! She has been like this since she realized you weren't in the house." Then I started crying again.

Jason came to the sofa, shifted me the baby so she was laying on his neck and chest. Then he put his other arm around me. He rocked us both saying over and over, "I am so sorry. I should have realized. Shhh. It's ok babies." We both fell asleep.

I slept a long time. Jason would wake me to use the bathroom, drink some soup and put me back to bed. He told me the baby woke up every 2 hours for a whole day to eat. She also refused to be put down. Every time he tried she would scream. When he held her, she grabbed his clothes for dear life.

Two days later at breakfast I asked Jason, "What did you mean when you said you should have known?"

"Separation Anxiety. We had a puppy that went through the same thing. It was weaned too young because the mother got ran over by a car. The pup cried for weeks for its mother. My little brother went through it too when Mom left on a business trip for the first time after he was born. I am so sorry. I just didn't realize she was so attached to me. I know how to fix the problem though. We'll test my solution and make sure it works for my before I leave again."

I spent more time playing with and caring for the baby. We also spent more time together as a trio, so she would get better used to me. When she would go to sleep we would put each of our shirts that we had been wearing that day in her crib with her. The baby would sleep fine and grip the shirts all night. I didn't change the shirts out when Jason was gone. But we put fresh ones every night when he came home. It worked.

I stayed home with the baby and Jason worked. He would go for a week or two and then be home for a week up to a month. He helped me get into night school, so that I could get my G.E.D. He helped me study, so I would pass my tests. He taught me how to protect myself and he worked with me, so I could be strong and stay fit.

We were together during my first Christmas of freedom. We went to Nevada and sold all my jewelry. He was against it, but I wanted to cut all the ties from my old life. I was never going back to my parent's home. If anything happened and he and I weren't together the money from the jewelry would help Angelica and me.

He insisted on carrying her in the removable car seat, so I carried the diaper bag. While in Nevada I found a new bag that I liked. My school bag was very old and practically falling apart.

I also found a present for Angelica. We walked by a shop that sold crystals. I showed Jason. "I want the snowflake because it's Christmas. Plus, snowflakes are unique like people are unique. Both made by God's own hand. I wanted it to be crystal so that when the sun kissed it, rainbows would appear. I want to hang it in her window at home. The rainbow is God's promise to never flood the world again. I want Angelica to know about God's promises and understand how God keeps his promises to us. God is love, and I want her to understand that."

"I don't know if I really believe in God. I have seen way too much of the evil that men do to each other."

"You must believe in God somewhere in your

heart. How else could you see so much evil and not give up and copy what you see? You are a good man and you told me that your mother sent you to Sunday school."

"Yeah, but I think that was just to give her a break from us three boys."

"Perhaps, but she may have had another reason. Did you ask her?"

"No."

"Perhaps she wanted you to make up your own mind. Perhaps she didn't want to force feed you religion, only to have you turn away. Maybe she just wanted to give you the choice to find your own faith your own way."

"I don't see evidence of your God anywhere."

"I see God everywhere."

"Look at what happened to you. Was that God's doing?"

"Some of it, yes, I believe it was. My sister Marta did her evil, my father his and Ruiz his. But me escaping, I couldn't have done it on my own. Ruiz didn't break my mind or my spirit. I believe God protected me. My dress being the same color as the grass. Alberto, a guard, helping me. I received no serious injuries when I escaped. I fell but didn't hurt the baby. I found a woman who is in law enforcement who got me out of the state. I met Tracy who needed to get to Florida when I needed someone to go there to protect Michelle. I met Lucy who introduced me to you. A good man who got me all the way to California. I see God's hand all over my life. Directing me, protecting me."

"Coincidence. Chance. Luck."

"That is an enormous amount of coincidence or chance. I should have won the lottery 10 times over with luck like that. You don't have to agree. It's ok. I can respect a difference of opinion. But all I ask is that you don't mock me for my beliefs."

"I wouldn't do that."

"I didn't think you would. But I hope you can understand how important it is for me to raise my daughter with God at the center of her life. Not religion, God. Can you agree to that?"

"I can live with that. If you want to go to church, I'll go with you. I want you to feel safe."

I grabbed his hand and squeezed. My eyes teared up. "Thank you. I thought about asking you, but I didn't want to make you uncomfortable."

"I'm here for you. Family, remember."

I paid for the crystal and we walked out into the street hand in hand. We stopped in another shop that sold teddy bears. He got a small one that Angelica could hold. He had it embroidered with the name Elvis. "My job is kind of dangerous sometimes and if anything happens to me I want her to know where her lullaby came from."

"Why don't you put your name on it?"

"If anything happens to me I don't want it to ever be a sad memory. I don't want it to be a memory of death. I want it to be a memory of joy and happiness."

"You will be careful, won't you? You will do your best to always come home to us."

"Yeah. I will always do my best to come home." His voice caught when he said it and he turned away. I pretended not to notice but my heart felt warmer somehow.

That Christmas was simple but lovely. I gave Jason an electric blue sweater that was very soft and looked very good on him. Jason gave me a crystal snowflake necklace on a silver chain. He said, "I want you to know I support you. I may not always agree with you, but I will at least try to understand your point of view."

I cried, and he held me. He has so much patience with me and the baby. I thank God, every day for Jason in my life.

Chapter 11: California? Nope!

Jason and I were in California for three months when disaster struck. Jason was in the apartment and I took Angelica with me in her stroller. I was doing a little middle of the week shopping. Bread from the bakery, cheese from the deli, things like that. I was paying more attention to the windows of the shops than my surroundings. So, it's my fault that we were almost kidnapped.

I was staring in a shop window when a man grabbed me by the arm. "Not far enough Maria. The boss wants to see you." It was a lovely warm day, but I suddenly felt like I was freezing. I recognized him at once as one of Ruiz's guards who held me in the shower. I never knew his name. All I could think was, *how did they find me*? I stayed where I was on the sidewalk with my mouth hanging open in shock. I started to shake. Tears filled my eyes. He yanked my arm and got my attention. "Get in the car." He started to pull me.

My vision blurred as the tears ran from my eyes. While I tried to think I moved slowly but acted like I was beaten and would do what I was told. I realized then that it was two men and neither one had a gun out. I quickly ran through the things that Jason had taught me, in my mind. *Disarm, Disable, Distance.* I grabbed the diaper-bag out of the stroller and put it on my back. I turned the stroller around to face me. He let go so I could grab the baby. I unbuckled Angelica, held my breath, and used the stroller to ram the man. I knocked him partway of the curb and he lost his balance and tripped and landed on the car with a shocked look on his face. I grabbed Angelica, prayed I hadn't hurt her and ran down the street and into a shop I knew had a back door. I heard shouting and cussing behind me. I stuck my right arm out and used it to barrel the door. I tried to slam it behind me, but I never looked back.

I ran out the back door and down the alley to an open back door. I heard gunshots as I ran inside. I ran through the restaurant and out the front door. I ran across the street and repeated the process. I did this for several streets. I tried not to think I held onto Angelica with my left arm and kept running using my right to knock things out of my way. I saw a cab and jumped in and told him to take me to the greyhound station. I told him he didn't let anyone stop him I would give him $100.00 in addition to the fare.

I constantly looked out the back window to see if I saw the car following us, but I never saw it. I got out at the greyhound and ran to the payphone. I called Jason and told him what happened. "How... Never mind. You remember what I told you if this ever happened?"

"Yes."

"Ok. I will meet you there in three days."

I had been upset when Jason first suggested that I keep $5000.00 of his money, all my money and a fake passport with me at all times. I thought he was being paranoid. Plus, the amount of money bothered me. Now I was so thankful that he had been cautious enough to plan ahead.

I got the next bus out of town. It was headed east. We stopped in Utah for a layover and I threw away my ticket and got a bus to Seattle, Washington. From there I took a cab to Lynden. It was a town near the Canadian Border. I could walk across the border through the woods if I had to hide.

I had the cab driver let me out at a

convenience store. I bought some ready to eat food for myself. I had enough diapers to last Angelica for at least four days. I was still breast feeding so she was ok for food.

But then I remembered reading that sometimes stress could dry your milk, so I got a bottle and some powdered formula just in case. I borrowed the telephone directory and found the hotel that was listed last. I checked in under the name Leticia Ramírez. If Jason didn't show up in three days I was supposed to cross over to Canada to Aldergrove. Another town close to the border.

Angelica cried and was fussy and seemed kind of scared. She slept even though Jason wasn't there, but I had to hold her the whole time. Her little hands gripped my shirt like she was afraid I would drop her. Jason showed up in two days. I was so relieved. We hugged and kissed briefly on the cheeks and he held Angelica and played with her for a while. She fell asleep in his arms, but he didn't put her down.

"How do you think they found us?" I asked.

"I don't know. Only one civilian knew we were going to California and Lucy didn't know exactly where."

"I'm worried about her and Michelle. What if he got to them somehow?"

"If he got to them there is nothing we can do. If he didn't and we contacted them we could lead him right to them. We have no choice. We have to stay away. Either way my name is mud. We are going to have to keep using false identities."

"What are we going to do?"

"For now, I took an emergency leave of absence. About 10 minutes after you called someone was busting down the door as I went out the window up the fire escape. I called the company once I was clear and I told them I was attacked and needed a cleanup crew. I didn't leave any bodies though."

"What took so long? Our go bags were already packed."

"I realized that we didn't have a go bag packed for Angelica. I grabbed her stuff and shoved it in the backup diaper bag. I can't believe I overlooked that."

"Not just you. Thank you so much for getting

her stuff but it wasn't worth your life. You should have just left it."

"No. I couldn't do that. She deserves her stuff as much as we do. It's not much."

"So, what else happened?"

"They knew my name. Called for me as I was going up the stairs. I got to the roof and used the pulley I rigged to get down to the ground as they were hitting the roof. Then set it on fire."

"Did it work like you planned?"

"Yep. Fire went north super quick and whole thing went up in about 10 seconds. Didn't even scorch the building." He looked so proud.

"Where do we go from here?"

"Anywhere we want." And we did. Jason checked me over. It turned out I had broken my arm during my escape. It wasn't until I was reunited with Jason that I calmed down enough to feel it or sleep. We went to the hospital and had my arm set.

We traveled around for 4 or 5 months. Jason checked in with the company regularly but refused to go in. They were putting more and more pressure on him. One day he just yelled,

"Well I have to take care of my family first! If you don't like it, you can fire me!!!" Then he hung up so hard I thought the phone might break.

Jason decided that we should stop in Oklahoma for a while. He left us there and took a short trip. He was gone for a week. I slept with one of his guns next to me the entire time. Angel slept in a drawer on the floor next to the bed.

CHAPTER 12: LOVE

It was after Angelica's first birthday that I knew I was in love with Jason. He was so gracious and kind with us. He was so patient. Such a wonderful father to Angelica. He never got tired of me asking questions about the world. I had missed so much while I was Ruiz's prisoner.

At first, I just thought we would be like brother and sister. Living together for mutual benefit. I never thought I would ever think about any man like a husband after everything I had been through with Ruiz. But I started to find that my heart skipped a beat whenever he was close. I started making excuses to sit next to him or be close enough to sniff him. I love the way he smells. His own clean, unique scent mixed with the soft leather from his jacket and the peppermints that he favors.

I found that when I looked at him to long I started to blush. My heart and breathing would speed up. I also found that he was looking at me differently. I didn't know what it meant, but it made me warm and tingly.

I didn't know if I could ever like the sex that goes on between men and women but for Jason I would put up with the pain. I decided to tell him. We put Angelica to bed and I told Jason that I wanted to speak with him. We sat on the couch facing each other.

I tried to speak very matter-of-factly. I had never done this before and I wasn't sure how to do this. "I wanted you to know that I am in love with you. I don't expect you to feel the same way. And I am not asking for anything. You will probably never feel for me what I feel for you and I have decided that I am ok with that. I don't know how I will do but if you want sex I give you permission and all I ask is that you try not to hurt me too much. I don't want Angelica to see bruises on me. I am not sure what normal sex is. I am sure that many of the things that Ruiz did to me were not normal, but I will try to please you. I just thought you should know."

At first, he looked very shocked, then he looked very angry. "I thought we were past this. I told you, you don't owe me anything. I don't expect you to trade yourself like that. I would never ask that of you. I do this because I lo.... care about you and Angel. Not because I expect anything in return."

He started to say I love you. I know he did. But does he mean love like family or love like lovers? "You don't believe me that I am in love with you do you?"

"No. I don't. I think you feel obligated to me and you are trying to make up for that."

"Obligated how? Because you had two colds in the last year and I had one. But you took care of me after that mess when you first left, and Angelica was up screaming for 3 days. So, I figure we are even for that. Us having to run, well that one is on me, but I warned you about what you would be in for."

"Well, everything, I guess. I thought at first it was just financially but who keeps track of colds? And for the record it was one cold and one exhausting mission that I almost didn't come back from because Jackson fucked up. That wasn't a cold."

"Ok. So, I do, but it looks like you do too. And as far as financially...." I left the room and got my diary and my money and brought them back and sat at the table. I looked up the figure to make sure I had it right. I counted out the money and marked paid in full at the bottom. I put the money for Jason in the spot that I wrote on to mark the place. I put the rest of the money in my pocket. I smacked him in the chest with the diary and he grabbed it. "In there is payback for every cent you ever spent on us. I tracked everything. I am no longer obligated to you for anything. And I am still in love with you, you idiot." I started pacing.

"I wasn't sure at first. Every time you come near me, my heart skips a beat. My favorite place to sit is next to you. I love the way you smell. I love all the considerate little things you do for both of us every day. When you touch me, or hold my hand, my body gets all warm and I get moist in my woman parts. And sometimes when you look at me, my body does things and I feel things I don't understand. I never thought I would want anyone to touch me after Ruiz. But I am having dreams of you doing things and I want those things with you. I wake up frustrated and feeling things, I don't understand and don't know how to fix. I don't know what to expect, but I do know that when there is pain, I would still do it for you because you are so important to me. I know that there is a lot I don't know. But I know how I feel. If you don't want me or don't feel the same way that's fine. But don't tell me how I feel. I love you." I left the room and went to the bathroom. I didn't want to wake Angelica and I was going to cry.

I don't know how long I was in there, but I wasn't done crying and there was a knock on the door. "Gabriella, will you come out here please?"

I sniffed and blew my nose. "In a minute." I tried to stop crying and put cold water on my face to try and make my eyes less puffy. I went back to the living room. "Yes?"

"Could you sit down please?" I did. "I have a lot to say. First, I'm sorry. I had no right to tell you how you feel. You have come a long way and I know you are a woman who knows her own mind. But, I was afraid. Knowing what you have been through, and you knowing what I do, I didn't think that you could ever love me. I was afraid to hope. I figured it was only a matter of time before you left me and took my world with you."

"Second, WOW, you kept **really** good notes. You have expenses on here that I didn't even remember getting until I saw them written down. You even have presents on here that I gave for birthdays or Christmas. I don't want the money. But I am going to take it because I know how you are. But only if you promise to stop keeping notes." I didn't say anything. Mostly because I couldn't. I was afraid if I spoke I would start crying. I saw how much he was hurt by the fact that I had kept notes and I had to look away. It made my heart ache. But I promised myself no matter what, no more keeping track. He put the diary down.

"I will take your silence to mean you will think about it. Third, I think I have loved you from the moment I saw you. You looked so vulnerable but were trying so hard to be brave. I definitely respected you. I think I knew for sure I was in love with you about 6 months ago when you and Angel were both sick. You were trying so hard to be a good Mom. You were healthy when I left to check in at work but eight hours later when I came back you were both miserable. The place was a wreck. You were covered in snot and baby food. There were tissues everywhere. You looked a wreck the baby was clean but obviously sick. You taped notes all over the walls for her medicine, your medicine, feeding times, bath times, friggin' everything you could think of, everywhere you could think of. And through all of it I thought you were so beautiful. I was so thankful to be with you. I even thanked God for you and Angelica being in my life. When you saw me, and your eyes lit up and you smiled so big. You didn't try to give me Angelica, but do you remember what you said? You said, 'I am so glad you made it home safe to us. I missed you so much. Are you hungry? I can cook dinner.' I knew then that you weren't just happy to see another pair of hands to help with the baby. You were glad to see me because of me. I still never dared to hope that you could ever love me." My heart soared! He loved me!

"I knew that you had the right to be free. Like everyone else. Free without anything hanging over your head. The idea of you with another man makes me crazy but I wanted you to have peace of mind. I went and talked to a lawyer and he hired a private investigator. I wanted you to know all of your options for getting away from Ruiz legally and permanently. I am still waiting to hear back. I used a false name to get the information, so it can't be traced back to us. I knew then I wanted to marry you. I want us to be forever. But if you don't want that too that's ok. I will take whatever you are willing to give me."

I felt like my heart would explode. I felt the tears rolling down my face. "No more keeping score. I love you and I trust you. I would love to marry you. But if we find out I am married to Ruiz I do not trust the courts to divorce us and protect my family. I would be married to you in my heart and face God with a clear conscience. I love you so much." I put my hands on his chest and put my ear over his heart. It was beating very rapidly.

"Six months ago, when you and Angelica were all better, I went out and got this ring made. If you ever left I was going to give it to you to remember me by. But now I just hope that will you marry me." He pulled a ring out of his pocket. It was a simple silver heart. My birthstone and Jason's were in the top and Angelica's was in the bottom. The stones were squares turned sideways and put together, so they looked like a heart inside the silver heart. On each side of the heart was a small diamond. On the outside of the band was a script inscription, *All My Love*. On the inside of the band it said, *Goes With You*.

I didn't say anything. I was crying to hard. I took the ring and put it on my finger. I grabbed

Jason by the face and pulled him down for a kiss. I kissed him so hard I forgot to breathe. I pulled away gasping and Jason started laughing. He grabbed me by the face, more gently than I had him, and started kissing me all over my face. Then he picked me up and twirled me around. My heart was fuller than I ever thought possible.

CHAPTER 13: I'M FREE

The answer came two weeks later. There was no Maria Gabriella Cortez with my birth date or social security number married anywhere in the America. That's why it took six months to find out.

When Jason told me, I didn't know how to feel. I suspected that it was all a lie from the beginning but to have proof, I think I was just in shock. They even checked every church registry in south Florida since I never left the state just in case.

In a strange way I don't think I felt a lot different. I realized, being with Jason, I didn't really care. I had meant what I said. I never felt married to Ruiz and knowing that I wasn't didn't change a lot for me. I would have lived with Jason forever even if I had been married to Ruiz.

But now that I know I am not married to that Demon it just made me realize I was already legally free. And **THAT** knowledge is what made me really happy. Jason and I could get married if we wanted to and it would be legal.

Jason and I were moving very slowly with the sex. Jason says that when you have sex with someone you love it should not hurt. All you should feel is pleasure after the virginity is no more. We kiss a lot and he touches me a little a time until he does something, and I freeze up. Then he stops and just holds me. Sometimes we talk. Sometimes I cry. Sometimes I get really mad.

I know he must be very frustrated. I told him we should just do it and I will get used to it. He was furious and told me to stop bringing it up. "Look. We will get there, but at your speed. I would rather jack off in the bathroom for the next 50 years than to know I caused you one moment of fear or pain." He had to take a minute to calm down.

He spoke softer now. "Gabriella. It will happen in time. You stay relaxed longer every time we fool around. You start things more often. You and I sleep in the same bed half the week now. Honey, it will happen in time. Stop trying to force it. I love you. That isn't going to change. I know what you went through, remember? Sometimes I stop because of the pictures running through _my_ head. One day there won't be a ghost between us anymore. We just have to give it time."

CHAPTER 14: TIME TO GO

Jason moved us back to California but two hours away from where he was assigned. He said we weren't going to be here long so just stay in the house until he came home. He said they claimed this assignment was crucial and he could write his own ticket, go anywhere he wanted. He would be gone for a week.

When he came home, I was shocked. Jason quit his job. He did his final debrief and turned in his paperwork. He said not everyone would know he left until Monday when it became official. He had them cycle the last of his pay into his retirement account, so he didn't have to worry about a paycheck or waiting on paperwork. He said we were leaving today. By the time his bosses figured out that he split that Friday, never to return we would be out of state.

I always told him, he didn't have to quit. He said he wanted to start our new life without blood on his hands.

We didn't have much. We didn't need much. Every place we stayed we made sure it was fully furnished. Everything we had fit into a couple of bags. We went from southern California to Chicago, Illinois in 2 days. He dropped us in a new apartment that he had already rented under a new name. He said he had been paying on it for 2 months already.

It was a cute little apartment in a brownstone building. It was a decent neighborhood near a church and a Catholic school. There was a park nearby with well-tended playground equipment.

He got groceries for us and took the van back to California. He said he would be gone about two weeks. He would be riding Greyhound several places then get off before his ticket stopped and hitchhike home to us. I worried the entire time he was gone.

When he finally got home he was happy and convinced that no one could follow our trail. I wasn't happy he hadn't told me about all of this, but I was glad we were safe.

About a month later he started his job as handyman for the Catholic church and school. He said he still wasn't convinced about God but with us in his life he was warming up to the idea.

Little by little our sex-life improved. We were finally able to "go all the way" about eight months after we got to Chicago. I didn't orgasm, but it didn't hurt, and it was pleasurable. Jason said I was fighting it. He thinks I was worried about making too much noise and waking Angelica. He was probably right.

Nearly a year after we moved to Chicago, we were married, quietly, by Father Sullivan under the names on Angelica's birth certificate. We asked him not to file it, all we cared about was being married before God. Legal paperwork was dangerous for us. Father Sullivan agreed. Jason had explained enough of our circumstances to him to convince him to marry us and keep quiet about it. As far as the rest of the congregation knew we were already married.

I didn't think I could ever be so happy as the day I found out my marriage to Ruiz was not real and I realized I was legally free. But today, marrying Jason, I felt like my heart would burst.

A part of me wished it could be my little girl dream, my family around me, a big party. Then I realized that the love between Jason, Angel and I is all I need. Our family is all I need. Well, maybe later, another baby. Mine and Jason's baby. Yes, I think that might be good for all of us.

Sister Mary Grace watched Angelica for us that night. It was the first time we had ever been away from her at the same time. It was the first time that we had been away from her overnight. But Angelica adored Sister Mary Grace. She had our number and Angelica had our undershirts from that day to sleep with. Plus, we were only blocks away.

Jason wanted us to go away for a Honeymoon, but it would have to wait until school let out for the summer. We took day trips all the time, but he wanted us to take a much longer trip. He said straight away that we would be taking Angelica with us. He is so protective of her.

Without having to worry about Angelica and trying to keep quiet I did feel more relaxed and more free-spirited. He asked how much I trusted him, and I told Jason, "I trust you with my heart, my mind, my body, my life and my soul."

He smiled and kissed me in a way that was different than before. It was more intense, more purposeful. I felt that feeling I get in my tummy that builds until I just can't let it go anymore and I make Jason stop. He said that is my threshold. That's when I fight the pleasure because I don't understand it.

"I love you and I believe you that you trust me. Angel isn't here. So, I am not going to stop this time. I will slow down but I want you to let go. Can you do that?"

I really thought about. "I don't know but I promise I will do my best."

"Just remember two things. I will never hurt you and screaming is ok. This is as close as you get to a rollercoaster without traveling to an amusement park."

I laughed until he put me on my back in the bed. He spread my legs and pinned me down. He did things to me with his mouth and hands that I had never imagined were possible. And I screamed. I screamed and moaned and begged. I begged for him not to stop. After that first orgasm he just held me and kissed me gently until I was calm. He got me a drink and started all over again.

I instantly became some kind of addict. I

wanted that feeling over and over. He never even put himself inside me that night. He spoke gently to me, whispering encouragement to get as loud as I want. He just gave me pleasure after pleasure until I finally passed out. I have never felt so loved, so happy, so treasured and so vulnerable in my life. In the back of my mind I was worried that I may have damaged his eardrums though.

By the time I woke up the next day it was after 10 o'clock. Jason was playing with Angelica in the living room. I got a shower and discovered parts of me were tender and a little sore. Not in a he hurt me way but like when you swim or play sports too long. You had fun but now you are a bit sore.

As I washed in the shower I discovered my body waking up and wanting more of the activities from the night before. I blushed all the way to the roots of my hair. I felt suddenly very shy.

When I walked in the living room I could swear he knew what I was thinking. I blushed harder and Jason laughed and looked ridiculously smug and pleased with himself. I tried to pretend not to notice and walked into the kitchen to get myself something to eat.

Jason came up behind me in the kitchen and wrapped his arms around me. He gently massaged my breasts and my nipples were hard as rocks in moments. "I made you a fruit salad. It's in the fridge." He parted my robe and gently played with the hem of my nightgown in the middle of my thighs. I shivered. He reached under my nightgown and cupped my woman's place and pulled me against his body. His manhood pressed against my lower back. He moaned a little. I was panting like a dog in summer. "I love you so much. I'm so glad you had fun last night." He used his left hand to pull my hair of my neck, so he could kiss it with his whiskery chin. I remembered that chin rubbing my thighs with his mouth in a more intimate place. I leaned into him harder and reached around and grabbed his bottom with both hands. I pulled him against me hard.

"We could put Angel down for a nap." I could hear the desperation in my voice and was shocked at it. When did I become this woman?

Jason chuckled. "Two hours early. She is not going to let that one slide. Beside you need food and fluids. When nap time comes we can pick up where we left off." He turned me around and kissed me. Not the intense one I was expecting but a gentle playful on the tip of my nose. "And don't worry love. I got you a special pillow. You can scream into it all you want to, and Angie will never hear you."

I felt suddenly clumsy. I slowly ate my breakfast, so I wouldn't spill and drank lots of water. I played with Angelica and Jason until nap time. I watched as he put her down and sang to her. She was asleep before the song ended, but he finished it anyway. My heart filled again with love for them both. I thanked God for all of my blessings. Jason picked me up and carried me to our bedroom. Then I thanked God for the pillow.

Over time, Jason taught me all about the ways of love between a man and a woman. And at my request he taught me how to make love to him with my mouth the way he makes love to me. At first, I was curious. But when I realized how much he enjoyed it, I felt and incredible sense of power. I got so good he had to use my pillow.

I discovered I liked being in control. Many times, I rode him like a derby pony and gloried in my power as a woman. I also discovered I liked to tease him. Little touches in the right place when no one was looking. Rubbing against him a certain way. He took to wearing oversized shirts to hide his almost constant arousal. "Just wait 'til we get home." Was all he ever said and walked as far away as possible with Angelica between us, so I would have a harder time teasing him. It didn't stop me. I liked the challenge.

When we took trips in the car we often had to take detours to find secluded spots. I teased him mercilessly whenever I wanted him inside me. He complied at every opportunity. We camped in the woods a lot. Away from regular campsites and other people. Angelica was a fantastically sound sleeper. And like most children fell asleep in the car easily.

I wanted another baby. But as often as we made love, unless he had the sperm count of Superman that wasn't going to happen. I did want a baby, but I just couldn't seem to stop. I wanted Jason more.

CHAPTER 15: A BLAST FROM THE PAST

We were blissfully happy in our marriage for over a year. Then one day we had and unexpected visitor. I was brushing Angelica's hair after her morning bath when there was a knock on the door. It had happened occasionally, neighbors asking for a cup of sugar, but we mostly kept to ourselves.

Jason opened the door and went stock still. "How the hell did you find me?"

"You would be surprised. Chance mostly. You were hard as hell to track down, do you know that?"

"Who knows I'm here? Who knows you're here?"

"Now is that any way to talk to your best friend?"

"Gabby, take her in the room please." I picked up Angelica and put her in her room. I told her to be very quiet and stay away from the window. She walked over to her shelf and started playing quietly with her toys.

I went back into the living room and took a

seat at the table facing the door like Jason taught me. Mr. Porter was sitting on the sofa.

"Gabby this man is Steven Porter. He is my oldest friend at my previous job. He is actually the one that recruited me. Steven this is my wife Gabby."

"Well, quite the looker. So, you're the reason that Jason quit."

"I never asked him to quit his job. That was his choice. He didn't tell me he was going to do it either. He just came home one day and said he had quit and we were moving. How did you find us Mr. Porter?"

"A mutual acquaintance of ours was in town on a research trip and just happened to spot Jason here, picking up some lumber. Baker was very surprised to see you. He knows how much I had been doing to try and find you and he followed you. You were very sloppy. Baker said you didn't even seem to notice the tail. He found out where you worked. Then did a little poking around. Found out where you live and here I am." Jason looked very angry. "So, Jason, I want you to come back to work for us. I will even give you the raise in pay you would have gotten if you stayed. What do you say?"

"No. I'm not going back to that again. I've made my peace with it. I'm out and I'm staying out."

"Now Jason. I know we've had these discussions and I know it bothers you. But the simple fact is you were born for this kind of work. Otherwise you wouldn't be so good at it. Why fight fate? Come on back." He looked around our cheaply furnished apartment. "It looks like you could use the money. Come on."

"No! Jason wasn't born to be a soldier. He was born to be his own man. He found his own place in this world away from war and we are happy. Leave us alone."

"Now little lady, Jason wasn't just a soldier. He was a very specific kind of soldier. And he was excellent at his job. A real artist. He has a talent for certain things, of shall we say, a delicate nature...."

"I know what he did. And I know who he is. Jason wanted away from that life and he is happy. If he wanted to go back I would support him in whatever he chose to do. But I really don't think he wants to go back to work for you. Do you Jason?" He looked so proud of me. He was grinning from ear to ear.

"No, I don't. Sorry Steve. I have no intention of going back to the company."

"Well, I am sorry to hear that. The offer will always be open if you ever change your mind. So, what's the little girl's name? What is she about three, four?"

"Her name is Angie. I think it's time for you to go now Steven."

"Gabby, is it? It was very interesting to meet you." He shook my hand, but I didn't like it. He left, and I told Jason that I thought we should move.

"Sweetie, you are just being paranoid. Steve is on the side of the good guys remember? I worked with him. I really think he will respect my wishes. He won't like it, but what can he really do?"

"Hmm. Have you seen Angelica's brush? I need to finish her hair." I spent the whole day looking and couldn't find it anywhere. For some reason it made me really uneasy. I told Jason that I thought Mr. Porter might have taken it.

"Why? What possible purpose could it serve?" We had no answers.

The next day we were walking to lunch in the city and I noticed a man looking at me. I don't know what got my attention, but he seemed very intent on me. I looked at him a little harder and realized he looked familiar but couldn't remember from where. I turned to get Jason's attention but when I tried to point him out he was gone. It made me very uneasy but, I couldn't say why.

That night I had a horrible nightmare and I woke up screaming. I remembered where I knew the man from. "Jason, it's Ruiz. The man. He was one of the guards for Ruiz."

"Sweetie, I don't think so. Ruiz's power and pull is mostly in Florida. Maybe he just looked like someone who worked for Ruiz." He rubbed my back trying to calm me down. I was still crying.

"I don't think so. I know he was a guard for Ruiz. If he's here Ruiz may not know where we are now, but he soon will. He'll come get us. He'll kill you. He...he..."

"Honey, calm down. You look very different than you once did. You are fuller, healthier. Your hair is a lot shorter and a different color than it was when you were with him.

Whenever we go out you wear hats or scarves and sunglasses. We have taken precautions. He's never seen Angelica. It's been almost two years since you saw anyone that worked for him."

"Oh God! My baby. My baby. The things he said he would do to her. He is EVIL! We have to leave."

"Gabriella! Calm down. It's going to be ok."

He held me while I cried. I thought I heard a sound in the hall, but Jason looked, and Angelica was in her room. When he checked on her she was crying. He brought her in and we all slept together that night.

Jason finally agreed with me that we should go. It was different when no one knew where we were but neither of us liked the fact that we had been exposed. We packed up and left the next day.

Jason was quiet for the next week while we traveled. We went everywhere. East, west, north, south. It didn't matter. We just went wherever the road took us. We never stayed anyplace longer than a week.

We traveled through Canada and Alaska

during the summer and went to a petting zoo for Angelica's fourth birthday. We spent the winter in a cabin in the back woods of Mississippi. It even had an outhouse. Once spring came we were on the road again.

"Maybe I should go back to working for my old job. I could get a protective detail on you two. Maybe they could even help us put him behind bars."

"Didn't you tell me you rejected that plan before we left California?"

"Yeah, but maybe I just wanted out so bad that I dismissed it before I really gave it all the thought it deserved. This is no way to live."

"I support you. I love you and I support you no matter what you decide."

We traveled for six more months. We settled in Michigan, but Jason saw someone he knew from the company after we had been there for only six weeks. We moved again. We changed cars. We changed our looks, even Angelica's.

We traveled for a few months. Then we went to Texas. We were there for two weeks. We were walking from the grocery store to the apartment trying to beat the rain. Suddenly someone was waiving at me from across the street. He was looking in the coffee shop window but waiving. When he faced me I saw Alberto, the guard who helped me escape from Ruiz. He was standing next to a car. He was mouthing something, but I couldn't make it out. Another man came out of the coffee shop and yelled at Alberto for being out of the car. He stopped mid-sentence and threw the coffee away and pulled his gun and started to chase us.

We dropped the groceries and ran up the stairs to the apartment and slammed and locked the door. We grabbed our go bags and I climbed in the dumbwaiter with Angelica. Jason was lowering us down and threw the bags on top. Then I heard him climb in and shut the door. He shoved a wedge in the door to help stop it from opening.

We got down to the first floor. I got out and Jason grabbed the bags from the top. He dropped them one at a time through the drop door he had made when we first got there. Then he got out and we grabbed our bags and ran out the door and in the alley. The sky opened up and rain came down in buckets.

I tried to shield Angelica. Then we heard

gunshots and Jason shoved me in front of him so both of our bodies would shield the baby. I picked her up and we ran. We kept running and sliding. Then it started to lightning and thunder. We ran into a parking garage and Jason broke a window and we stole a car and got the Hell out of there.

"How do they keep finding us?! It doesn't make sense!" Jason said nothing, but his face was so tight I thought he was going to break his teeth. We drove straight through to just outside Las Vegas. We drove the car about 500 feet into the desert and Jason used some torn clothing to make a fuse and blew up the car.

We walked the two miles into town and got a cab to the Greyhound. We didn't talk. Jason went and bought the tickets and we waited for our bus. "You're going, back, aren't you?"

"Yes. Do you hate me?"

"No. I love you."

"I just..." I put my finger on his lips.

"I know. You are just doing what you think you need to do to protect us. And I love you." My eyes filled with tears. I didn't want him to have to go back to killing but he was doing it to protect us.

CHAPTER 16: KIDNAPPED

Jason rejoined the company. He took a pay cut instead of a raise so that when he was out of town we would have a protection detail. We have been back in California for a while now and have not seen anyone who works for Ruiz.

Mr. Porter thinks that Ruiz might have had two cars doing something called tag team tailing. Using car phones to communicate with each other and trade off regularly so we wouldn't get suspicious. Why he waited to try and grab us, Mr. Porter had no theory for. Unless they were afraid of Jason.

The only good thing about Jason being gone is that it gives him a chance to build up his sperm count. I am hoping to get pregnant soon. Angelica is almost five and I think it's a good time to start diapers again.

He just got home yesterday, and he was gone for two weeks. Jason said he is going to be gone for two months this time. I hate it. I know how much this is wearing on him. He said this time they are going to put a female agent in the house with me and Angelica.

We will also have our male agent when we go outside. I don't like having these people in my home. A few of them made Angelica really nervous and I had to talk to Mr. Porter and get someone else. It annoyed him, but he did it.

I am so proud of my little girl. She is doing so well. Her teacher is very impressed as well. Ms. Delaney says Angelica helps the other children when her work is done.

I am so excited for Jason to come home tomorrow. We have missed him so much. I can't wait to tell him about the new baby. I put a teddy bear on the bed for him to see when he comes home. It says Elvis on the tummy. I wonder if he will get it right away or if he will have to think about it a while.

Amanda got a call today and said she had to go. Jacobs our male guard says he will go to the park with me and Angelica today. He makes Angelica nervous, but Mr. Porter says there is no one else who can come today. Jacobs promised to keep his distance, so Angelica will relax.

We all got to the park and Angelica went to play with her friends. Jacobs kept his word and stayed about 200 feet away from us at all times. I sat on a bench at the far end of the rest of the mothers. Some women smoked, and I didn't like the smell.

Angelica was on the swings when I felt cold metal on the back of my neck. "I underestimated you once, I won't do it again. Get up!" I didn't move. I looked around for Jacobs. I almost gave up hope but then I saw him on the other side of the playground.

As soon as he saw me he smiled turned around and walked away. "Ha, ha, ha. Good old Jacobs. He works for us but refuses to get his hands dirty." I felt chilled to the bone. I did the only thing I could do. I got up and started walking away. "Hey! Where are you going?"

"You have me. I admit defeat. I am assuming you have a car. Where is it?"

"Not so fast. Point out the girl."

"No."

"Point out the kid. Ruiz wants you both."

"No."

"I mean it." He pushed the gun into my neck. It hurt but I refused to cry out. Ruiz had done far worse. "Point out the kid!"

"Or what you'll shoot me? If you shoot me, you don't get either one of us. I will not let Ruiz get my daughter. Kill me if you must or take me alone."

He thought about it. I started to pull away and that made up his mind. He grabbed me by one arm and the other man he was with grabbed me by the other arm and pointed a gun at me also. I closed my eyes and let them lead me. I prayed for my daughter. I prayed for Jason and I prayed for our child in my belly. I felt the tears roll down my face.

Suddenly I heard Angelica cry, "Momma! Momma!" I didn't respond, and I didn't speed up.

"Is that yours?"

"No." I kept walking.

"Momma! Momma!" That was too close. I yanked away from the men and turned around.

"NO! Run! Get away! DANGER!" I saw Angelica fall. I saw in her face that she understood. I fought and clawed and hit anything I could. Screaming the whole time. Several parents were looking around and realizing there was a big problem.

One man grabbed me around the waist and held on tight. I hit and clawed and screamed, trying to get away the whole time. Finally, he just threw me on the ground and held me there. He was too big for me to push off.

The other man was running for Angelica. She got up and ran back toward the playground screaming, "HELP! HELP ME!" She ran fast for her age, but the man caught up with her and grabbed a fist full of her hair and stopped her.

Some of the parents started to run toward Angelica but the man started shooting a gun in the air above the other children's heads. People started running around trying to grab their kids and get out of the park. The man picked up Angelica and she started screaming harder and kicking and scratching.

She put up a good fight. I was proud of her. He yelled at her but in the chaos, I couldn't understand what he said. Angie stopped fighting and just cried.

He brought her back to us. The second man let me up but kept the gun on me. The first man handed Angie to me and told me to walk or he would shoot her in the knee. They took us to a brown car and made us get in the trunk. They got in the car and started driving.

To Be Continued....

Please look for the next book in The Devil's Daughter Series, Book 2: Angelica

CHAPTER 17: HELP

Letter from the Author to the Reader:

I understand being afraid to ask for help from the people or organizations around you. I grew up in an abusive household. My biological father was in the military and friends with a lot of the local police. Many of whom were just as perverted as he was. I spent a lot of time in the streets. As dangerous as it was I felt I was safer there then in my house. I have been homeless. I have been hopeless. I have been suicidal. I was made into a victim before I was out of diapers.

Eventually I got out. I wanted to be "normal." I wanted to not feel the way I felt. I wanted to stop hurting. I thought when I got away the hurting would just stop. It didn't. I figured out pretty quick that "normal" didn't really exist. There was a general average depending on where you live or how you lived. But "normal" was a lie.

I think at first that scared me more than anything. How do I reach a goal that doesn't exist? How did I learn to be average? What could make my memories go away? Answer: Nothing.

I read self-help books. I read religious books. I talked with people. I tried to get my biological father prosecuted for what he had done to me. I found closed door after closed door. Eventually I made a friend that recommended therapy. I ignored the suggestion for a long time. Looking back now, many wasted years. Finally, I tried therapy and my world changed drastically for the better.

But, it's different now. There are so many organizations, and people who want to help and have the resources to do so.

Take a chance. Call a number or contact help online. You have to be willing to take that step and help yourself. Courage is being afraid and doing something anyway.

I have seen so many lives ruined by fear and abuse. The best thing I ever did for myself was get the help I needed to become the person I am. I believe myself to still be a work in progress. However, I am happier and healthier than I have ever been. My relationships with my friends and family, that I have contact with, are in a very healthy place. Therapy does work if you put in an honest effort. It took me several years to get to a good enough place that I could carry on, on my own. If I had it to do over again I would have started therapy sooner.

If you or someone else needs help, **please** get the help you need. Things are very much different now than when I was growing up. There are more people who want to help you than there were 35 years ago, heck than even 20 years ago. Please take care of yourself by getting the help you need. You're worth it.

Hotlines - USA

If you are experiencing a medical emergency, are in danger, or are feeling suicidal, call 911 immediately.

Suicide Hotline: 800-784-2433
Immediate Medical Assistance: 911
Crisis Call Center: 800-273-8255 or text ANSWER to 839863

Teen Health & Wellness: Real Life, Real Answers is for educational purposes only. If you have a question on a health or wellness issue, we strongly encourage you to call one of the hotlines below to speak to a qualified professional or speak to a trusted adult, such as a parent, teacher, or guidance counselor.

Listed below are hotlines, help lines, and information lines, organized by subject. These national organizations can also refer you to state and local services in your community.

AIDS and HIV

Rape, Sexual Violence, and Domestic Violence

Alcohol and Drugs

School Violence

Bullying and Cyberbullying

Sexuality and Sexual Health

Depression

Stress and Anxiety

Eating Disorders

Suicide

Grief and Loss

Teen Parenting

Homelessness and Runaways

Teen Pregnancy

Mental Health

AIDS and HIV

AIDS info
800-HIV-0440 (800-448-0440)   12 p.m. to 5 p.m. EST, Monday to Friday
http://www.aidsinfo.nih.gov

Canadian AIDS Society
HIV Information Hotlines:
http://www.cdnaids.ca/resources/hiv-information-hotlines/

Crisis Text Line
Text HELLO to 741741 or message us at facebook.com/CrisisTextLine to chat with a Crisis Counselor.
Twenty-four hours a day, seven days a week

Kids Help Phone (Canada only)
800-668-6868 Twenty-four hours a day, seven days a week http://www.kidshelpphone.ca

HIV/AIDS Hotlines by State
https://hab.hrsa.gov/get-care/state-hivaids-hotlines

Hope Line
Call or text 919-231-4525 or 1-877-235-4525
https://www.hopeline-nc.org/

National AIDS Hotline
800-CDC-INFO (232-4636) Twenty-four hours a day, seven days a week
https://www.cdc.gov/hiv/

Ontario Online and Text Crisis and Distress Service (ONTX) Text 741741 from 2 p.m. to 2 a.m. daily Twenty-four-hour distress and crisis lines: 416-408-HELP (4357)

Project Inform: National HIV/AIDS Treatment Hotline
800-822-7422 or 415-558-9051 in the San Francisco Bay Area 7 a.m. to 1 p.m. EST, Monday to Friday
http://www.projectinform.org

Teen Line
(310) 855-HOPE (4673) (800) TLC-TEEN (852-8336) (U.S. and Canada only) Or text TEEN to 839863 6 p.m. to 10 p.m. Pacific Time, every night https://teenlineonline.org

Alcohol and Drugs

Al-Anon/Alateen
888-425-2666 8 a.m. to 6 p.m. EST, Monday to Friday
https://al-anon.org/newcomers/teen-corner-alateen/

Crisis Call Center
800-273-8255 or text ANSWER to 839863
Twenty-four hours a day, seven days a week
http://crisiscallcenter.org/substance-abuse/

Crisis Text Line
Text HELLO to 741741 or message us at
facebook.com/Crisis Text Line to chat with a
Crisis Counselor.
Twenty-four hours a day, seven days a week

Hope Line
Call or text 919-231-4525 or 1-877-235-4525
https://www.hopeline-nc.org/

Kids Help Phone (Canada only)
800-668-6868   Twenty-four hours a day,
seven days a week
http://www.kidshelpphone.ca

**The National Alcohol and Substance Abuse
Information Center** 800-784-6776 Twenty-
four hours a day, seven days a week
http://www.addictioncareoptions.com

**National Institute on Alcohol Abuse &
Alcoholism**
800-662-HELP (4357) Twenty-four hours a
day, seven days a week
http://www.niaaa.nih.gov

**Ontario Online and Text Crisis and Distress
Service (ONTX)** Text 741741 from 2 p.m. to 2
a.m. daily   Twenty-four-hour distress and
crisis lines: 416-408-HELP (4357)

Teen Line
(310) 855-HOPE (4673)   (800) TLC-TEEN
(852-8336) (U.S. and Canada only) Or text
TEEN to 839863   6 p.m. to 10 p.m. Pacific
Time, every night https://teenlineonline.org

Thursday's Child National Youth Advocacy Hotline
800-USA-KIDS (800-872-5437)   Twenty-four
hours a day, seven days a week
http://www.thursdayschild.org

Bullying and Cyberbullying

Bullying UK (UK only)
0808-800-2222   Twenty-four hours a day,
seven days a week http://www.bullying.co.uk

Canadian Association for Suicide Prevention
Find crisis centers in your area:
https://suicideprevention.ca/need-help/

Crisis Call Center
800-273-8255 or text ANSWER to 839863
Twenty-four hours a day, seven days a week
http://crisiscallcenter.org/crisisservices-html/

Crisis Text Line
Text HELLO to 741741 or message us at

facebook.com/Crisis Text Line to chat with a Crisis Counselor. Twenty-four hours a day, seven days a week

Cyber Tip line
800-843-5678 Twenty-four hours a day, seven days a week
http://www.cybertipline.com

Hope Line
Call or text 919-231-4525 or 1-877-235-4525
https://www.hopeline-nc.org/

Kids Helpline (Australia only)
1-800-55-1800 Twenty-four hours a day, seven days a week
http://www.kidshelp.com.au

Kids Help Phone (Canada only)
800-668-6868 Twenty-four hours a day, seven days a week
http://www.kidshelpphone.ca

Lesbian Gay Bi Trans Youth Line (Canada)
1-800-268-9688 or text 647-694-4275
http://www.youthline.ca/

Ontario Online and Text Crisis and Distress Service (ONTX)
Text 741741 from 2 p.m. to 2 a.m. daily Twenty-four-hour distress and crisis lines: 416-408-HELP (4357)

National Suicide Hotline
800-SUICIDE (784-2433)800-442-HOPE
(4673) Twenty-four hours a day, seven days a
week http://www.hopeline.com

National Suicide Prevention Lifeline
800-273-TALK (8255) Twenty-four hours a
day, seven days a week
http://www.suicidepreventionlifeline.org

Thursday's Child National Youth Advocacy Hotline
800-USA-KIDS (800-872-5437) Twenty-four
hours a day, seven days a week
http://www.thursdayschild.org

Teen Line
(310) 855-HOPE (4673) (800) TLC-TEEN
(852-8336) (U.S. and Canada only) Or text
TEEN to 839863 6 p.m. to 10 p.m. Pacific
Time, every night https://teenlineonline.org

The Trevor Lifeline (U.S. only)
866-4-U-TREVOR (488-7386) Twenty-four
hours a day, seven days a week
http://www.thetrevorproject.org

Your Life Iowa: Bullying Support and

Suicide Prevention

(855) 581-8111 (24/7) or text TALK to 85511
(4–8 PM every day) Chat is available Mondays–
Thursdays from 7:30 PM–12:00 AM
http://www.yourlifeiowa.org

Depression

Canadian Association for Suicide Prevention
Find crisis centers in your area:
https://suicideprevention.ca/need-help/

Crisis Call Center
800-273-8255 or text ANSWER to 839863
Twenty-four hours a day, seven days a week
http://crisiscallcenter.org/crisisservices-html/

Crisis Center and Hotlines Locator by State
https://suicidepreventionlifeline.org

Crisis Text Line
Text HELLO to 741741 or message us at
facebook.com/Crisis Text Line to chat with a
Crisis Counselor. Twenty-four hours a day,
seven days a week

Depression and Bipolar Support

800-273-TALK (8255) Twenty-four hours a day, seven days a week
http://www.dbsalliance.org

Hope Line
Call or text 919-231-4525 or 1-877-235-4525
https://www.hopeline-nc.org/

Kids Help Phone (Canada only)
800-668-6868 Twenty-four hours a day, seven days a week http://www.kidshelpphone.ca

Lesbian Gay Bi Trans Youth Line (Canada)
1-800-268-9688 or text 647-694-4275
http://www.youthline.ca/

National Hope Line Network
800-SUICIDE (784-2433)800-442-HOPE (4673) Twenty-four hours a day, seven days a week http://www.hopeline.com

Ontario Online and Text Crisis and Distress Service (ONTX) Text 741741 from 2 p.m. to 2 a.m. daily Twenty-four-hour distress and crisis lines: 416-408-HELP (4357)

Suicide Prevention Services Depression Hotline

630-482-9696 Twenty-four hours a day, seven days a week http://www.spsamerica.org

Teen Line
(310) 855-HOPE (4673)   (800) TLC-TEEN (852-8336) (U.S. and Canada only) Or text TEEN to 839863   6 p.m. to 10 p.m. Pacific Time, every night https://teenlineonline.org

Thursday's Child National Youth Advocacy Hotline
800-USA-KIDS (800-872-5437)   Twenty-four hours a day, seven days a week http://www.thursdayschild.org

Your Life Iowa: Bullying Support and Suicide Prevention
(855) 581-8111 (24/7) or text TALK to 85511 (4–8 PM every day) Chat is available Mondays–Thursdays from 7:30 PM–12:00 AM
http://www.yourlifeiowa.org

Eating Disorders

Crisis Call Center
800-273-8255 or text ANSWER to 839863 Twenty-four hours a day, seven days a week http://crisiscallcenter.org/crisisservices-html/

Crisis Text Line
Text HELLO to 741741 or message us at
facebook.com/Crisis Text Line to chat with a
Crisis Counselor.   Twenty-four hours a day,
seven days a week

Hope Line
Call or text 919-231-4525 or 1-877-235-4525
https://www.hopeline-nc.org/

Kids Help Phone (Canada only)
800-668-6868 Twenty-four hours a day, seven
days a week http://www.kidshelpphone.ca

**National Association of Anorexia Nervosa
and Eating Disorders** 630-577-1330   10
a.m. to 6 p.m. EST, Monday to Friday
http://www.anad.org

National Eating Disorders Association
800-931-2237 9 a.m. to 5 p.m. EST, Monday
to Friday
http://www.nationaleatingdisorders.org

**Ontario Online and Text Crisis and Distress
Service (ONTX)** Text 741741 from 2 p.m. to 2
a.m. daily Twenty-four-hour distress and
crisis lines: 416-408-HELP (4357)

Teen Line
(310) 855-HOPE (4673)   (800) TLC-TEEN
(852-8336) (U.S. and Canada only) Or text
TEEN to 839863   6 p.m. to 10 p.m. Pacific
Time, every night https://teenlineonline.org

Thursday's Child National Youth Advocacy Hotline
800-USA-KIDS (800-872-5437)   Twenty-four
hours a day, seven days a week
http://www.thursdayschild.org

Grief and Loss

Crisis Call Center
800-273-8255 or text ANSWER to 839863
Twenty-four hours a day, seven days a week
http://crisiscallcenter.org/crisisservices-html/

Crisis Text Line
Text HELLO to 741741 or message us at
facebook.com/Crisis Text Line to chat with a
Crisis Counselor.   Twenty-four hours a day,
seven days a week

Hope Line
Call or text 919-231-4525 or 1-877-235-4525
https://www.hopeline-nc.org/

Kids Help Phone (Canada only)

800-668-6868 Twenty-four hours a day, seven days a week
http://www.kidshelpphone.ca

National Hope line Network
800-SUICIDE (784-2433)800-442-HOPE (4673)   Twenty-four hours a day, seven days a week http://www.hopeline.com

National Mental Health Association Hotline
800-273-TALK (8255)   Twenty-four hours a day, seven days a week http://www.nmha.org

Ontario Online and Text Crisis and Distress Service (ONTX)   Text 741741 from 2 p.m. to 2 a.m. daily Twenty-four-hour distress and crisis lines: 416-408-HELP (4357)

Teen Line
(310) 855-HOPE (4673)   (800) TLC-TEEN (852-8336) (U.S. and Canada only) Or text TEEN to 839863   6 p.m. to 10 p.m. Pacific Time, every night https://teenlineonline.org

Tragedy Assistance Program for Survivors (TAPS)
800-959-TAPS (8277)   Twenty-four hours a

day, seven days a week http://www.taps.org

Thursday's Child National Youth Advocacy Hotline

800-USA-KIDS (800-872-5437) Twenty-four hours a day, seven days a week
http://www.thursdayschild.org

Your Life Iowa: Bullying Support and Suicide Prevention

(855) 581-8111 (24/7) or text TALK to 85511 (4–8 PM every day) Chat is available Mondays–Thursdays from 7:30 PM–12:00 AM
http://www.yourlifeiowa.org

Homelessness and Runaways

Boys Town National Hotline - serving all at-risk teens and children

800-448-3000 Twenty-four hours a day, seven days a week
Text VOICE to 20121, every day, 2 p.m. to 1 a.m. CST http://www.boystown.org/hotline

Crisis Call Center

800-273-8255 or text ANSWER to 839863
Twenty-four hours a day, seven days a week
http://crisiscallcenter.org/crisisservices-html/

Crisis Text Line
Text HELLO to 741741 or message us at
facebook.com/Crisis Text Line to chat with a
Crisis Counselor. Twenty-four hours a day,
seven days a week

Hope Line
Call or text 919-231-4525 or 1-877-235-4525
https://www.hopeline-nc.org/

Kids Help Phone (Canada only)
800-668-6868 Twenty-four hours a day, seven
days a week http://www.kidshelpphone.ca

National Runaway Switchboard
800-RUNAWAY (786-2929) Twenty-four
hours a day, seven days a week
http://www.1800runaway.org

**Ontario Online and Text Crisis and Distress
Service (ONTX)** Text 741741 from 2 p.m. to
2 a.m. daily Twenty-four-hour distress and
crisis lines: 416-408-HELP (4357)< /p>

Teen Line
(310) 855-HOPE (4673) (800) TLC-TEEN
(852-8336) (U.S. and Canada only) Or text
TEEN to 839863 6 p.m. to 10 p.m. Pacific
Time, every night https://teenlineonline.org

Thursday's Child National Youth Advocacy

Hotline
800-USA-KIDS (800-872-5437) Twenty-four
hours a day, seven days a week
http://www.thursdayschild.org

Mental Health

Crisis Call Center
800-273-8255 or text ANSWER to 839863
Twenty-four hours a day, seven days a week
http://crisiscallcenter.org/crisisservices-html/

Crisis Text Line
Text HELLO to 741741 or message us at
facebook.com/Crisis Text Line to chat with a
Crisis Counselor.   Twenty-four hours a day,
seven days a week

Hope Line
Call or text 919-231-4525 or 1-877-235-4525
https://www.hopeline-nc.org/

Kids Help Phone (Canada only)
800-668-6868 Twenty-four hours a day, seven
days a week
http://www.kidshelpphone.ca

National Hope line Network
800-SUICIDE (784-2433)800-442-HOPE
(4673)   Twenty-four hours a day, seven days a
week http://www.hopeline.com

National Institute of Mental Health Information Center

866-615-6464   8 a.m. to 8 p.m. EST, Monday to Friday

http://www.nimh.nih.gov/site-info/contact-nimh.shtml

National Mental Health Association Hotline

800-273-TALK (8255)   Twenty-four hours a day, seven days a week http://www.nmha.org

Ontario Online and Text Crisis and Distress Service (ONTX)   Text 741741 from 2 p.m. to 2 a.m. daily Twenty-four-hour distress and crisis lines: 416-408-HELP (4357)

Teen Line

(310) 855-HOPE (4673)   (800) TLC-TEEN (852-8336) (U.S. and Canada only)   Or text TEEN to 839863   6 p.m. to 10 p.m. Pacific Time, every night https://teenlineonline.org

Thursday's Child National Youth Advocacy Hotline

800-USA-KIDS (800-872-5437) Twenty-four hours a day, seven days a week

http://www.thursdayschild.org

Your Life Iowa: Bullying Support and Suicide Prevention
(855) 581-8111 (24/7) or text TALK to 85511 (4–8 PM every day) Chat is available Mondays–Thursdays from 7:30 PM–12:00 AM
http://www.yourlifeiowa.org

Rape, Sexual Violence, and Domestic Violence

Child help USA National Child Abuse Hotline
800-4-A-CHILD (422-4453)   Twenty-four hours a day, seven days a week
https://www.childhelp.org

Crisis Call Center
800-273-8255 or text ANSWER to 839863
Twenty-four hours a day, seven days a week
http://crisiscallcenter.org/child-abuse-reporting/

Crisis Text Line
Text HELLO to 741741 or message us at facebook.com/Crisis Text Line to chat with a Crisis Counselor. Twenty-four hours a day, seven days a week

Hope Line

Call or text 919-231-4525 or 1-877-235-4525
https://www.hopeline-nc.org/

Kids Help Phone (Canada only)
800-668-6868 Twenty-four hours a day, seven days a week
http://www.kidshelpphone.ca

Love is respect, National Teen Dating Abuse Helpline
(866) 331-9474 Twenty-four hours a day, seven days a week
http://www.loveisrespect.org

National Domestic Violence Hotline
800-799-SAFE (7233)   Twenty-four hours a day, seven days a week http://www.ndvh.org

Ontario Online and Text Crisis and Distress Service (ONTX)   Text 741741 from 2 p.m. to 2 a.m. daily Twenty-four-hour distress and crisis lines: 416-408-HELP (4357)

Rape, Abuse, and Incest National Network
800-656-HOPE (4673)   Twenty-four hours a day, seven days a week http://www.rainn.org

Safe Horizon's Rape, Sexual Assault &

Incest Hotline

Domestic Violence Hotline: 800-621-HOPE
(4673)   Crime Victims Hotline: 866-689-HELP
(4357)   Rape, Sexual Assault & Incest
Hotline: 212-227-3000   TDD phone number
for all hotlines: 866-604-5350 Twenty-four
hours a day, seven days a week
http://www.safehorizon.org

Teen Line

(310) 855-HOPE (4673)   (800) TLC-TEEN
(852-8336) (U.S. and Canada only) Or text
TEEN to 839863   6 p.m. to 10 p.m. Pacific
Time, every night https://teenlineonline.org

Thursday's Child National Youth Advocacy Hotline

800-USA-KIDS (800-872-5437) Twenty-four
hours a day, seven days a week
http://www.thursdayschild.org

Your Life Iowa: Bullying Support and Suicide Prevention

(855) 581-8111 (24/7) or text TALK to 85511
(4–8 PM every day) Chat is available Mondays–
Thursdays from 7:30 PM–12:00 AM
http://www.yourlifeiowa.org

School Violence

Crisis Call Center
800-273-8255 or text ANSWER to 839863
Twenty-four hours a day, seven days a week
http://crisiscallcenter.org/crisisservices-html/

Crisis Text Line
Text HELLO to 741741 or message us at
facebook.com/Crisis Text Line to chat with a
Crisis Counselor. Twenty-four hours a day,
seven days a week

Hope Line
Call or text 919-231-4525 or 1-877-235-4525
https://www.hopeline-nc.org/

Kids Help Phone (Canada only)
800-668-6868 Twenty-four hours a day, seven
days a week
http://www.kidshelpphone.ca

**National Center for Mental Health
Promotion and Youth Violence Prevention**
9 a.m. to 5 p.m. EST, Monday to Friday
http://www.promoteprevent.org

**Ontario Online and Text Crisis and Distress
Service (ONTX)** Text 741741 from 2 p.m. to
2 a.m. daily Twenty-four-hour distress and

crisis lines: 416-408-HELP (4357)

SPEAK UP
866-SPEAK-UP (773-2587)   Twenty-four
hours a day, seven days a
week http://www.bradycampaign.org/our-
impact/campaigns/speak-up

Teen Line
(310) 855-HOPE (4673)   (800) TLC-TEEN
(852-8336) (U.S. and Canada only) Or text
TEEN to 839863   6 p.m. to 10 p.m. Pacific
Time, every night https://teenlineonline.org

**Thursday's Child National Youth Advocacy
Hotline**
800-USA-KIDS (800-872-5437) Twenty-four
hours a day, seven days a week
http://www.thursdayschild.org/

Sexuality and Sexual Health

American Sexual Health Association
919-361-8488 8 a.m. to 8 p.m. EST, Monday
to Friday http://www.ashastd.org

Canadian AIDS Society
HIV Information Hotlines:
http://www.cdnaids.ca/resources/hiv-information-hotlines/

Centers for Disease Control (CDC) INFO
800-CDC-INFO (232-4636) Twenty-four hours a day, seven days a week http://www.cdc.gov

Crisis Call Center
800-273-8255 or text ANSWER to 839863
    Twenty-four hours a day, seven days a week
http://crisiscallcenter.org/crisisservices-html/

Crisis Text Line
Text HELLO to 741741 or message us at facebook.com/Crisis Text Line to chat with a Crisis Counselor. Twenty-four hours a day, seven days a week

Hope Line
Call or text 919-231-4525 or 1-877-235-4525
https://www.hopeline-nc.org/

GLBT National Youth Talk line
800-246-PRIDE (7743) 4 p.m. to 12 a.m. EST, Monday to Friday 12 p.m. to 5 p.m. EST, Saturday

http://www.glnh.org/talkline

Kids Help Phone (Canada only)

800-668-6868 Twenty-four hours a day, seven days a week http://www.kidshelpphone.ca

Lesbian Gay Bi Trans Youth Line (Canada)

1-800-268-9688 or text 647-694-4275 http://www.youthline.ca/

National AIDS Hotline

800-CDC-INFO (232-4636) Twenty-four hours a day, seven days a week https://www.cdc.gov/hiv/

Ontario Online and Text Crisis and Distress Service (ONTX) Text 741741 from 2 p.m. to 2 a.m. daily Twenty-four hour distress and crisis lines: 416-408-HELP (4357)< /p>

Planned Parenthood National Hotline

800-230-PLAN (7526) - for routing to local resources   Twenty-four hours a day, seven days a week http://www.plannedparenthood.org

Teen Line

(310) 855-HOPE (4673)   (800) TLC-TEEN (852-8336) (U.S. and Canada only) Or text TEEN to 839863   6 p.m. to 10 p.m. Pacific Time, every night https://teenlineonline.org

Thursday's Child National Youth Advocacy Hotline
800-USA-KIDS (800-872-5437)   Twenty-four hours a day, seven days a week
http://www.thursdayschild.org

Trans Lifeline
U.S.:(877) 565-8860   Canada: (877) 330-6366
This hotline is staffed by volunteers who are all trans identified and educated in the range of difficulties transgender people experience. Operators are generally available twenty-four hours a day, seven days a week.
http://www.translifeline.org

Stress and Anxiety

Crisis Call Center
800-273-8255 or text ANSWER to 839863
Twenty-four hours a day, seven days a week
http://crisiscallcenter.org/crisisservices-html/

Crisis Text Line
Text HELLO to 741741 or message us at facebook.com/Crisis Text Line to chat with a Crisis Counselor. Twenty-four hours a day, seven days a week

Hope Line
Call or text 919-231-4525 or 1-877-235-4525

https://www.hopeline-nc.org/

Kids Help Phone (Canada only)
800-668-6868 Twenty-four hours a day, seven days a week
http://www.kidshelpphone.ca

National Institute of Mental Health Information Center
866-615-6464 8 a.m. to 8 p.m. EST, Monday to Friday
http://www.nimh.nih.gov/index.shtml

National Mental Health Association Hotline
800-273-TALK (8255)   Twenty-four hours a day, seven days a week
http://www.nmha.org

Ontario Online and Text Crisis and Distress Service (ONTX)
Text 741741 from 2 p.m. to 2 a.m. daily Twenty-four-hour distress and crisis lines: 416-408-HELP (4357)

Teen Line
(310) 855-HOPE (4673)   (800) TLC-TEEN (852-8336) (U.S. and Canada only) Or text TEEN to 839863   6 p.m. to 10 p.m. Pacific

Time, every night https://teenlineonline.org

Thursday's Child National Youth Advocacy Hotline

800-USA-KIDS (800-872-5437) Twenty-four hours a day, seven days a week
http://www.thursdayschild.org

Your Life Iowa: Bullying Support and Suicide Prevention

(855) 581-8111 (24/7) or text TALK to 85511 (4–8 PM every day) Chat is available Mondays–Thursdays from 7:30 PM–12:00 AM
http://www.yourlifeiowa.org

Suicide

Canadian Association for Suicide Prevention

Find crisis centers in your area.
https://suicideprevention.ca/need-help/

Crisis Call Center

800-273-8255 or text ANSWER to 839863
Twenty-four hours a day, seven days a week
http://crisiscallcenter.org/suicide-prevention/

Crisis Text Line

Text HELLO to 741741 or message us at facebook.com/Crisis Text Line to chat with a

Crisis Counselor. Twenty-four hours a day, seven days a week

Hope Line
Call or text 919-231-4525 or 1-877-235-4525
https://www.hopeline-nc.org/

Kids Help Phone (Canada only)
800-668-6868   Twenty-four hours a day, seven days a week
http://www.kidshelpphone.ca

National Suicide Hotline
800-SUICIDE (784-2433)800-442-HOPE
(4673) Twenty-four hours a day, seven days a week http://www.hopeline.com

National Suicide Prevention Lifeline
800-273-TALK (8255)   Twenty-four hours a day, seven days a week
http://www.suicidepreventionlifeline.org

Ontario Online and Text Crisis and Distress Service (ONTX) Text 741741 from 2 p.m. to 2 a.m. daily   Twenty-four-hour distress and crisis lines: 416-408-HELP (4357)

Teen Line
(310) 855-HOPE (4673)   (800) TLC-TEEN
(852-8336) (U.S. and Canada only) Or text

TEEN to 839863   6 p.m. to 10 p.m. Pacific Time, every night https://teenlineonline.org

Thursday's Child National Youth Advocacy Hotline
800-USA-KIDS (800-872-5437) Twenty-four hours a day, seven days a week
http://www.thursdayschild.org

Your Life Iowa: Bullying Support and Suicide Prevention
(855) 581-8111 (24/7) or text TALK to 85511 (4–8 PM every day) Chat is available Mondays–Thursdays from 7:30 PM–12:00 AM
http://www.yourlifeiowa.org

Teen Parenting

Baby Safe Haven
Confidential toll-free hotline: 888-510-BABY (2229)
Safe Haven Infant Protection Laws enable a person to give up an unwanted infant anonymously. As long as the baby has not been abused, the person may do so without fear of arrest or prosecution. State finder map: http://safehaven.tv/states

Boys Town National Hotline - serving all at-risk teens and children 800-448-3000
Twenty-four hours a day, seven days a week Text VOICE to 20121, every day, 2 p.m. to 1 a.m. CST
http://www.boystown.org/hotline

 Crisis Text Line
Text HELLO to 741741 or message us at facebook.com/Crisis Text Line to chat with a Crisis Counselor. Twenty-four hours a day, seven days a week

Hope Line
Call or text 919-231-4525 or 1-877-235-4525
https://www.hopeline-nc.org/

Kids Help Phone (Canada only)
800-668-6868 Twenty-four hours a day, seven days a week http://www.kidshelpphone.ca

Ontario Online and Text Crisis and Distress Service (ONTX) Text 741741 from 2 p.m. to 2 a.m. daily Twenty-four-hour distress and crisis lines: 416-408-HELP (4357)

Postpartum Support International
800-944-4PPD (4773) Calls returned within 24

hours http://postpartum.net

Teen Line
(310) 855-HOPE (4673) (800) TLC-TEEN
(852-8336) (U.S. and Canada only) Or text
TEEN to 839863 6 p.m. to 10 p.m. Pacific
Time, every night
https://teenlineonline.org

Teen Pregnancy

American Pregnancy Helpline
866-942-6466 Twenty-four hours a day,
seven days a week http://www.thehelpline.org

Baby Safe Haven
Confidential toll-free hotline: 888-510-BABY
(2229)
Safe Haven Infant Protection Laws enable a
person to give up an unwanted infant
anonymously. As long as the baby has not
been abused, the person may do so without
fear of arrest or prosecution. State finder
map: http://safehaven.tv/states

Birthright International
800-550-4900 Twenty-four hours a day,
seven days a week http://www.birthright.org

Crisis Call Center

800-273-8255 or text ANSWER to 839863
Twenty-four hours a day, seven days a week
http://crisiscallcenter.org/crisisservices-html/

Crisis Text Line

Text HELLO to 741741 or message us at
facebook.com/Crisis Text Line to chat with a
Crisis Counselor. Twenty-four hours a day,
seven days a week

Hope Line

Call or text 919-231-4525 or 1-877-235-4525
https://www.hopeline-nc.org/

Ontario Online and Text Crisis and Distress Service (ONTX) Text 741741 from 2 p.m. to 2 a.m. daily Twenty-four-hour distress and crisis lines: 416-408-HELP (4357)

Planned Parenthood

800-230-PLAN (7526) - for routing to local
resources   Twenty-four hours a day, seven
days a week
http://www.plannedparenthood.org

Teen Line

(310) 855-HOPE (4673)   (800) TLC-TEEN
(852-8336) (U.S. and Canada only) Or text
TEEN to 839863   6 p.m. to 10 p.m. Pacific

Time, every night   https://teenlineonline.org

Thursday's Child National Youth Advocacy Hotline
800-USA-KIDS (800-872-5437) Twenty-four hours a day, seven days a week
   http://www.thursdayschild.org

"Resources Recommended by Teen Health & Wellness" Last Updated: November 2017

ABOUT THE AUTHOR

I was born in 1973. Due to the extreme abuse I went through as a child I was unable to have children of my own. I would like to foster or adopt but due to my current financial state I can't yet.

I have always had a passion for writing but never had the confidence in myself to put my work out there. My friends (my adopted family) kept encouraging me to submit my work but I was afraid it just wasn't good enough. I thought if I don't try I can't fail. Wrong. By not trying I was cheating myself. It took me a long time and a lot of pushing from my family to do it. I decided to publish through Amazon because I thought it was the best fit for me for my first book. I hope you enjoy my work.

www.ingramcontent.com/pod-product-compliance
Lightning Source LLC
Chambersburg PA
CBHW060827120626
46557CB00001B/399